MISTRESS OF HERSELF
GEORGIE'S STORY

MISTRESS OF HERSELF
GEORGIE'S STORY

LADIES OF INDEPENDENCE BOOK ONE

EVELYN RICHARDSON

CAVEL
PRESS

Kenmore, WA

CAMEL PRESS

A Camel Press book published by Epicenter Press

Epicenter Press
6524 NE 181st St.
Suite 2
Kenmore, WA 98028

For more information go to:
www.Camelpress.com
www.Coffeetownpress.com
www.Epicenterpress.com
www.evelynrichardson.net

Cover design by Scott Book
Interior design by Melissa Vail Coffman

Georgie's Story
Copyright © 2024 by Evelyn Richardson

ISBN: 978-1-68492-214-7 (Trade Paper)
ISBN: 978-1-68492-215-4 (eBook)

Library of Congress Control Number: 2024931756

Many thanks to colleagues Jennifer Webb and Cathie Sanford Ghorbani who generously let me borrow family names for Captain Kincade Webb and Viscount Sanford

ACKNOWLEDGMENTS

To the fabulous members of Regency Fiction Writers who generously share their knowledge no matter how minute or obscure.

PROLOGUE

"THANK YOU, MY LORD." LADY GEORGIANA CLAVERTON pinned a polite smile on her face as Lord Weatherleigh returned her to her brother after the quadrille. It was late in the Season and the air in Almack's ballroom was stifling, but then, Georgie, only daughter of the Duke of Roxburgh and reluctant participant in the rituals of the *ton*, found Almack's stifling even in the dead of winter.

"Pompous toad," she muttered under her breath to her partner's retreating back.

"Georgie!" Her brother Freddy's tone might be shocked, but his eyes were sympathetic. He knew his sister was as bored by the Season in London as he was intrigued by it, but then, he was the Marquess of Wrothingham, heir to the Duke of Roxburgh, free to indulge himself in his penchant for beauty and style with an enormous collection of exquisite snuff boxes, intricately tied cravats, and waistcoats that took the observer's breath away. His sister, on the other hand, was forced to endure the platitudes of partners eager to win the hand of the daughter of one of England's most influential and wealthy peers. Poor Georgie, whose love of horses and country life was equal to her elder brother's obsession with fashion and *objects d'art*, resented time spent in the rarified atmosphere of London at the height of the Season. She begrudged every hour passed away from the freer, horse-filled existence of the family estate, only accepting the torture of balls and routs in the name of family duty.

Freddy was also experienced in that misery, having been betrothed since birth in a longstanding family arrangement to a lady of overweening arrogance until he was saved by the Earl of Linton. The earl had forced Lady Lavinia Harcourt to cry off by threatening exposure of her attempt on her sister-in-law's life. Lavinia had considered this prospective sister-in-law to be a threat to, or at least an evil influence on Freddy. Even after Lord Adrian Claverton and Juliette de Flournoy had married, Lavinia had done her best to avoid Juliette. She considered Juliette soiled by her residence in London's most elite seraglio. Even the fact that Juliette was the daughter of the Comte de Flournoy and descended from one of France's most noble and revered families was tainted by her being *in trade*, as the owner of Maison Juliette, the *ton's* most sought-after modiste. Yes, Freddy understood and sympathized with anyone faced by the prospect of a suffocating future under the thumb of a rigorously demanding partner.

"But Freddy, he is a complete fraud, swanning around on that flashy chestnut of his which any fool can see is too mis-proportioned even to qualify as a cart horse, much less the thoroughbred he claims it to be, and because I am a mere female, he treats me as though my attics are to let if I don't praise his mount to the skies."

Freddy nodded; his blue eyes troubled. If his sister had been an Incomparable, she would have been treated with all the reverence she deserved, but being *a great gawky girl*, as a former modiste had called her, she was regarded critically by men who were unnerved by a face that bespoke character rather than beauty, and by its animated expression, with eyes that saw too much and a chin that hinted at determination and perseverance. They refused look beyond to see the lively and intelligent woman underneath. It was a rare man who was self-assured enough to evince interest in Lady Georgiana Claverton, despite her impressive pedigree and immense fortune. It was a great deal too bad, Freddy mused as he searched in vain for such a person in the crowded ballroom. Georgie deserved the happiness of someone who understood and appreciated her, like the loving companionship that made his brother Adrian light up whenever his eyes lighted on Juliette. For himself, Freddy knew he could hope for no such thing. Heirs to dukedoms could not marry for love, but he could hope for such a thing for his sister and his other brother, the Reverend Lord

John Claverton of St. George's, Hanover Square.

At this moment, Georgie's thoughts were focused less on escaping boring partners and more on finding one for Freddy. Now that he had been rescued from the clutches of *Medusa*, as Georgie always thought of Lady Lavinia, he needed someone who not only understood her brother's passion for beauty, but encouraged him in that passion. Just recently, inspired by the exquisite wood brought from India on the Earl of Linton's ship, and encouraged by his successful design of a looking glass for Maison Juliette, Freddy had ventured to suggest some design ideas for furniture being crafted by George Oakley, a cabinet maker in Bond Street. Much to Freddy's delight, his ideas had been accepted, and Georgie wanted to find someone for Freddy who could appreciate and share in his delight.

Georgie glanced around the room, a sly smile stealing across her lips as she caught sight of her dear friend, Lady Verena Carstairs, conversing in a corner with her mother and another woman Georgie did not recognize. Lady Verena was even less enamored of evenings at Almack's than Georgie which, coupled with a shy and retiring nature that was absolutely foreign to the ebullient Georgie, meant she was unlikely to find anyone who would appreciate her quiet intelligence. For Verena, this suffering on the marriage mart was an utter waste of time, unless . . .

Georgie turned to her brother, summoning up her most winning smile. "Freddy, be a dear and ask Lady Verena to dance. I shall go talk to her mother while you do."

Knowing his sister, Freddy mistrusted the deceptively sweet and utterly uncharacteristic tone. He fixed her with a highly skeptical look, quite out of character for the soft-hearted Freddy.

"Don't be a nodcock, Freddy. You know she is my dearest friend, and you know you could make the *ton* sit up and take notice of her with just one dance, not to mention what it will do for her confidence. It is not that she lacks spirit, it's that she rates her attractions so low. Just look what wearing creations from Maison Juliette has done for her."

Freddy followed his sister's gaze. It was true that since her costuming had been taken over by Maison Juliette, Georgie's friend had lost most of her mousey look. Her bearing was more assured, her movements, once hesitant, could almost be called graceful.

"Be sure to ask her about her gardens at Carstairs Hall. That will make her quite animated, which is always a good thing where *tonnish* observers are involved. Now come along!" Georgie linked her arm through her brother's with a determined tug.

"And here I didn't think you noticed, much less cared for, such things like who danced with whom, or whether they were or animated or not," Freddy grumbled good-naturedly as he followed his sister towards the Carstairs women.

The son of the Duke of Roxburgh never had to concern himself with whether or not he was considered worthy of notice by the *ton*; he just was. Even if he'd been born an idiot without a penny to his name, someone desperate for a title would have considered him a desirable catch. But Freddy had a tender heart, and he knew what it meant not to be appreciated for who he truly was, to have his interests and passions dismissed as utterly irrelevant, so he bowed gracefully over Lady Verena Carstairs' hand and begged her for the honor of the next dance.

He was amply rewarded for his kindness when, following his sister's instructions, he asked his partner about her gardens. He was astonished and impressed at her wealth of knowledge, not only about the plants and flowers, but about the layout that showed each plant to its best advantage. They became so immersed in their discussion, that, unaware the dance had ended, they remained chatting until the surrounding couples had left the floor.

"Thank you, Lady Verena," Freddy bowed over her hand as he restored her to her mother. "I can safely say I have never enjoyed such an enlightening dance."

"You are too kind, my lord. I do appreciate a stimulating conversation and I am also most sensible of the honor you have conferred on me by asking me to dance."

It was gratefully spoken, but Freddy saw the twinkle in her eye as she acknowledged his generosity, and he liked her the more for it. She might be timid and shy, but she was awake on all suits, and definitely a fount of knowledge where gardens were concerned. Of course, he should have known there was more to her than met the eye or his sister would not have wasted a moment of her time and thought on her.

Then revelation dawned. Freddy's betrothal had been such an ironclad part of his life that matchmaking had never entered the picture, but now he was free, and it occurred to him that matchmaking might become very much a part of his life, possibly being practiced this very moment by his nearest and dearest. He shot a suspicious glance in Georgie's direction, but she was deep in conversation with Lady Carstairs, apparently oblivious to the fact that the dance was over.

In fact, Georgie was very much aware, not only that the dance had ended, but of the way her brother and Verena had lingered talking after it, and she was doing her level best not to hug herself with glee as she forced herself to pay some semblance of attention to Lady Carstairs' plan for their return to Carstairs Hall at the end of the Season which was fast approaching.

CHAPTER 1

O N THE WAY HOME IN THE CARRIAGE that evening, Georgie congratulated herself on the success of her stratagem, but there was very little else she could do to throw her brother and friend together again, as not only the Carstairs, but everyone else in the *ton*, was deserting London for the country. Usually this was the best part of the Season for Georgie—the moment she climbed into the carriage to head home to Claverton—and the irony of having found a project that inspired her just as she was about to leave for Cambridgeshire was not lost on her. This time, however, she would not be heading to Claverton, but to her brother Adrian's estate near Newmarket for an extended stay with her brother and sister-in-law and her nephew, Auguste, who, at almost five was already begging his father for a pony. Truly, he was a child after his horse-mad father and aunt's own hearts.

Having barely survived the carnage at Waterloo, Lord Adrian Claverton had returned home to devote his life to raising the best racing thoroughbreds England could produce, and his sister, avid horsewoman that she was, never tired of hanging around the stables listening to grooms, stable-boys, other breeders, and the veterinarian, Mr. Tripp, talk of all things horse. It was balm to Georgie's soul after a Season holding herself in check as she dutifully, if reluctantly, followed her mother from one stifling function to another. It was not that the Duchess of Roxburgh was unsympathetic. She was as uncomfortable with the constraining rituals of the *ton* as her daughter, but she knew her duty, both as a wife to one of the country's political leaders, and mother of one of England's most noble and ancient families, so she reluctantly left her dogs—most of them who were as dear to her as horses were to her daughter—and endured the Season to ensure the next generation carried on their splendid heritage.

Now Georgie was free! Free to indulge in galloping around the countryside to her heart's content and spending the rest of her time in the stable. As the carriage pulled away from Claverton House the next morning and rounded the corner of Grosvenor Street, Georgie heaved a sigh of relief as she looked forward to feasting her eyes on green fields, congenial company, and a life unfettered by a constant changing of costumes. Juliette and Adrian were cordial to their neighbors, but these social encounters were confined to relatively intimate dinners where people talked of country matters, which were much more to Georgie's taste than the gossip of the *ton*.

That evening Juliette had arranged for a simple family meal to be served after the traveler had arrived and refreshed herself, but first there was Auguste to be fussed over. He had been allowed to stay up well past his bedtime to greet his aunt, but despite the arrival of a favorite family member, the boy was nodding and heavy-eyed when nurse brought him to greet Georgie. The sleepiness vanished, however, the instant she produced a long paper-wrapped package from behind her back.

"For me?" He reached out eager arms as nurse set him down.

"Yes. Open it." Georgie undid the string as he pulled away the paper to reveal a hobby horse.

"You are a devil," her brother growled, "now we are in the basket! I shall never hear the end of it."

"See Papa?" Mounting the horse Auguste bounced over to his father. "I can ride it, so now may I have a pony?"

"As I said," Adrian shook his head at his sister. "You shall pay for this. Auguste knows you are nearly as good a rider and judge of horseflesh as I am so I shall refer him to you whenever he plagues me about a pony or riding lessons."

"I think it is a lovely present, and more appropriate than the real thing at his age." Juliette patted her husband's shoulder.

"You underestimate my sister . . . and Auguste." Adrian shot Georgie a look. "This is only the beginning of her campaign to make me dance to her and Auguste's tune, just as she is doing with poor dear Freddy who has only just escaped from under the cat's paw."

"Freddy?" Juliette glanced at her sister-in-law who had the grace to look conscious.

"See?" Adrian pointed an accusing finger at Georgie. "Ask her about her friend Lady Verena Carstairs. Yes, dear sister, our brother John happened to write to me that Freddy has suddenly been considering improving the gardens at Wrothingham Abbey. Having spent years putting off marriage to Lady Lavinia with the excuse of his improving projects, now that he is free of her, why is he so concerned with the gardens? It appears he had an inspiring conversation at Almack's with a young woman who happens to be a gardening expert. See," he turned to his wife as Georgie's conscious look deepened, "None of us is safe from my sister's machinations."

"I was only trying to help," Georgie protested. "Neither one of them is properly appreciated for their talents so I threw them together so they could appreciate one another. Where is the harm in that?"

"What did I tell you?" Adrian's fixed his wife with a look of foreboding. "It is only the beginning. Soon she'll have us all dancing to her tune. Oh, she smiles innocently enough, but my sister is a dangerous woman, I tell you."

"Then let us hope she can exert her formidable powers on Mrs. Selwyn who insists she has business so *urgent* that she must call on me tomorrow." Juliette sighed, "She means well, but I do find her compulsion to whip us all into shape exhausting. However," Juliette threw her sister-in-law a challenging smile, "since Georgie has the same compulsion, perhaps she can beat Mrs. Selwyn at her own game."

"I do *not* whip people into shape!" Georgie was indignant. "I merely help them get what they want or . . . well, show them what they need," she amended in the face of her brother's incredulous stare

"At any rate, you can help me stave off whatever industrious project for which the Empress of the County wants to recruit me." Juliette gave Georgie an encouraging smile.

"Certainly." Georgie was secretly in awe of her brother's wife, who not only fulfilled her obligations as Lady Adrian Claverton with grace and charm, but also owned and ran Maison Juliette, the *ton's* most fashionable modiste. That was what Georgie wanted to do. She did not

want to be someone's wife or mother; she wanted to do something of
her own, something useful, something people would recognize as the
direct product of her skill. She still remembered the early days at Maison
Juliette when Juliette had let her help set the shop to rights. She'd been so
proud and happy sweeping, dusting, polishing, and even contributing a
few useful items from the lumber room at Claverton House. Those days
working with Juliette's fellow ladies from Mrs. Gerrard's, London's most
exclusive seraglio, had been the most gratifying Georgie had ever known,
and she was bound and determined to make a life for herself where she
would always feel that way. For the moment, however, she would do her
level best to support her sister-in-law in the onslaught of Mrs. Selwyn.

The Squire's lady was exactly what one would have expected from
someone who saw it as her duty to insure the proper functioning of
the surrounding countryside. From an old county family, she had the
appropriate sense of entitlement and self-assurance to be the consort
of the hard-riding Squire whose family, like his wife's, had established
themselves-well before the Conquest.

It turned out that Mrs. Selwyn was not calling on Lady Adrian so
much to recruit her services as to complain about the newest member
of the neighborhood. "It is an American, er *gentleman*," she remarked
with a sneer that set the feathers in her bonnet quivering in indignation
as she took the most commodious chair in the drawing room. "He has
inherited Clinton House from his father who was apparently related to
the Clintons through some distant connection." The Squire's lady sniffed
derisively at the heretofore respectable Clintons who had suddenly
demonstrated an utter lack of taste by being related to an American.

"Clinton House!" Georgie's eyes lit up. "Such a lovely old place." She
remembered first discovering it on one of her rides and had fallen in love
with the ancient bridge across the moat and the tower entrance.

"Well, it is utterly ruined now that it is in the hands of that upstart."

"You have met him, then, I take it," Juliette inquired using the soothing
tones she usually saved for Auguste in his most fractious moments.

"No, I have not!" her guest snapped. "And after I so graciously invited
him to call on me."

Commanded, more like, Georgie thought. As someone who also
disliked being told what to do, she sympathized heartily with Clinton
House's new owner.

"He sent a note, a *note*, mind you, begging my pardon, saying he was leaving for London the next morning."

"Well, then, perhaps he will call on his return."

But Juliette's reasonable suggestion seemed only to infuriate her guest more. "No respect for his betters, or for manners," Mrs. Selwyn snorted.

And how does this American know she's his better? Georgie wondered. She was beginning to like this unknown person more and more. Not only did he own an enchanting estate, but he had put the officious busybody into a state of high dudgeon without even trying. It seemed as though Georgie's visit to Cambridgeshire was going to be more interesting than anticipated.

"And is there something you would like me to do?" Juliette prompted, knowing full well that any encounter with the Squire's lady never failed to require some sort of effort on Juliette's part.

"The very thing! Of course I shall not ask him to call again, but we need to know something more about the fellow so the neighborhood can be properly warned."

"I dare say." Juliette hid a smile, "I shall consult with my husband and see what can be done. "And how does he call himself?"

"Excellent." Their guest rose. "He is a Mr. Justin Appleton. Now I must be gone. The vicar's wife is simply incapable of arranging the altar flowers without me there to guide her." And with that, Mrs. Selwyn departed as precipitately as she had arrived.

CHAPTER 2

"AND THERE YOU HAVE IT," JULIETTE CHUCKLED, "our work is cut out for us. Do you suppose if we invited him to join us for dinner rather than demanding he account for himself that Mr. Justin Appleton might actually favor us with his company? I do wonder if he truly had business in London or was so put off by the royal summons that he decided the acquaintance was not worth the effort. I hear these Americans are quite strong-minded and not easily seduced by mere social standing."

"I would find myself hard-pressed not to avoid such an obvious command, and I am English, and a mere female at that. I hope he realizes the fortuitousness of his escape." Georgie shook her head. "If Adrian pens a note, I can ensure that Ned will deliver it, as we always include Clinton House in our daily gallop. And I promise I will hang back unobtrusively and let Ned hand over the note," she added in the face of Juliette's skeptically raised eyebrow. "I won't even try to discover anything about him." But Georgie could see that her sister-in-law was not convinced. It was unfortunate that Juliette knew her so well, but there it was.

The next day Georgie did restrain her impulse to ride over the bridge with Ned and through the towered portico of Clinton House, instead, hovering dutifully out of sight for which she was amply rewarded as no one appeared to be answering the door. She could just see Ned waiting patiently under the portico for any signs of life, none of which appeared, when a loud banging erupted from one of the outbuildings off around the corner on her side of the moat.

Glancing around to make sure she was unobserved, Georgie urged Nero toward the sound, dismounting just to the side of a large open door of what looked to be a blacksmith's. Who would need their own smithy when Mr. Smith and his son Tim ran such an excellent one in the village? Georgie dismounted and, securing Nero, she approached slowly though there was no need for such caution as the man at the anvil was oblivious to anything but his work.

Georgie, however, was not oblivious; she was mesmerized by powerful shoulders, sweat-darkened auburn hair clinging to a sculpted brow over deep-set eyes, a strong nose, and a determined jaw. Her mouth went dry as the man raised his hammer and the damp shirt plastered itself against an impossibly broad chest. She swallowed convulsively. What was wrong with her? Men were nothing to her! She had laughed as her schoolmates sighed over the dancing master; she had dismissed with scorn the admiring comments her acquaintances whispered to one another over this or that tulip of the *ton*; she had considered deluded those she heard gushing over a handsome face or someone with *an air about him*. Now she was standing in a forge weak-kneed over a stranger while she suddenly comprehended the look in Juliette's eyes when they lighted on her husband. So that was what it was all about!

"May I help you?" A deep voice interrupted these disturbing and unwelcome revelations.

"Ah . . . er yes, I rang at the door, but no one seemed to be about. I have a message for your master."

"Old Bentley is rather deaf I am afraid, and the maids . . ." he shrugged those magnificent shoulders, his infectious grin revealing dazzlingly white teeth. Truly she had lost her mind, for who noticed teeth, or even cared? He held out a grimy hand whose dirt could not obscure its capable strength.

"Um," Georgie cast about desperately for an excuse, any excuse, not to hand over the expected and nonexistent note.

He inspected her curiously for a moment, then took pity on her, withdrawing his hand. "I shall have my master call on yours if you will but give me his direction."

"Er, yes, Ashbourne Hall, er Lord Adrian Claverton." Georgie remained transfixed, unable to tear herself away as he nodded, then, picking up his hammer, returned to his work. But what was his work? Not a horseshoe, but a small wheel with lots of what looked like teeth. What was he making? Georgie opened her mouth to ask, then, realizing that a servant didn't ask questions like that, shut it with a snap. "Thank you."

She turned and fled back to Nero who, having found a spare patch of grass, was munching contentedly. She searched for something to stand on, finally using the steps of another outbuilding to fling herself into the saddle and hurried back toward the bridge just as Ned crossed back across the moat.

"Sorry, my lady. I would not rouse anyone."

"Don't trouble yourself. I met a field hand and instructed him to invite his master to call on my brother." It was not quite the truth, but near enough, and Georgie was not about to examine why she did not want to admit or think any further about what had really happened.

Justin Appleton's grin widened as he turned back to his work. That was one intriguing woman, and whoever she was, she was *not* a servant. It was curious though that she had not bridled or reacted in the least when he had assumed out loud that she was one. He had known from the first that she wasn't, and he had just been trying to provoke her with his reference to her master, but she wouldn't be provoked—admirable in anyone, but especially in a well-bred young woman. Justin Appleton might be an American, but he recognized *the quality* when he saw them: the self-assured posture, the distinctive articulation, and that riding habit! What servant wore a riding habit? I was not just an ordinary habit. Yes, the lines were simple, almost to the point of plainness, emphasizing the wearer's superb figure and arresting features. It was not a beautiful face, but it was a mesmerizing one, with the bright blue eyes full of lively intelligence and curiosity, and a nose and jaw that spoke of abundant character. Yes, the habit's design was purposely uncomplicated, but the cloth, though drab, was of the richest quality, and the construction superb. As an engineer, Justin appreciated good design and construction anywhere, be it a bridge, a road, a carriage, or even a riding habit.

Justin Appleton's visitor had been a woman of distinction, there was no doubt of that. But what was she doing calling on him? Was she investigating him to see for herself who and what the American was, unlike the Squire's wife who had commanded his obeisance. She was curious, his unexpected visitor, and not only about Justin Appleton. He had watched her examining the gear he was laboring over and seen the struggle it cost her not to ask him about it.

He had also seen the way her breath caught as she took in his jacket-less torso and sweat—dampened shirt, and observed the shock, immediately followed by a flicker of annoyance, that had registered in her eyes as it sank in on her that Justin Appleton was a fine figure of a man.

It was that flicker of annoyance at herself that had really intrigued him. Instead of focusing on him with a flirtatious batting of eyelashes as so many women did, her eyes had turned inquisitively to the gear on the anvil. That annoyance showed character. How many people had the fortitude to be critical of themselves? And the attention to his work betrayed a questioning and active mind. All in all, Justin's nameless visitor presented a tantalizingly complex personality, for anyone, much less a woman.

But Justin Appleton did not have time for women, even intriguingly complicated ones. In a few weeks he was going to visit the famous engineer Thomas Telford, and he needed something to present to England's premier bridge and canal builder to prove the seriousness of his interest—something like a lock paddle that would not, when reaching a certain position, tear the windlass out of an inattentive lock-keeper's hands—hence the gear he hoped would counteract that.

Having inherited a Hudson River shipping business from his recently deceased adoptive father, Justin was bound and determined to carry on the man's dream of building a canal that would connect the Hudson River, and the Atlantic Ocean, to all the fertile lands in Ohio and beyond, linking trade from New York City to Detroit, and Thomas Telford was the man to teach him how. Justin had heard in great detail about British canal construction from his father's friend and his personal hero Robert Fulton whom he had met when Fulton was developing his steamboats on the Hudson. It was Fulton, who had met the Duke of Bridgewater himself and his engineer in whose steps Telford was following, who had inspired Justin's stepfather and Justin with the Erie Canal project. Justin didn't want to invest just money in the canal, he wanted to contribute engineering skill and knowhow, to be intimately involved in the construction of what was sure to be a modern marvel.

The completion of a dream this big meant he had no time for any distractions, even an intriguing young woman who was not the servant she allowed him to think she was. With that, Justin put her out of his mind and went back to work.

CHAPTER 3

Fate, however, was against Justin, for Lady Georgiana Claverton was not so easily dismissed.

Two days after encountering the mysterious young woman, Justin decided he should make a visit to Ashbourne Hall, just in case the story about a message from Lord Adrian Claverton was the truth.

He had not ridden a mile down the road toward Lord Adrian's estate when he heard the sound of raised voices around the bend ahead of him. ". . . very ill and needs care. I shall purchase him from you if you refuse to take care of him yourself," a woman's voice insisted.

"You interfering bitch! You will do nothing of the sort, you miserable trollop!"

Justin rounded the curve just as the rider of a horse ahead of him raised his whip to crack it across the shoulders of a young woman standing at the horse's head, stroking its nose with one gentle hand while clasping the reins of her own magnificent black mount in the other.

Justin urged Brutus forward, jumped down, wrenched the offensive rider from the saddle and delivered a well-placed blow to the man's jaw.

"Oh well done! Excellently done!" His mystery woman grinned, clapping her hands as her assailant collapsed at her feet in an inanimate heap.

"My lady, my lady, whatever is amiss?" A red-faced groom, gasping for breath, burst around the bend from the other direction to join them. "Oh, my lady, you should not ride so far ahead, you know. Bess cannot keep up with Nero."

"Calm yourself, Ned. All's well that ends well. This kind gentleman took care of the situation most expertly." Ned's mistress turned to acknowledge her rescuer. Her eyes widened. "Oh, I . . ."

"I believe we have met before, Lady . . .? I gather you must somehow be related to Lord Adrian Claverton."

She had the grace to look sheepish, but only for a moment before the determined chin rose. "Lady Georgiana Claverton, sister to Lord Adrian. And I thank you for helping me out, but this . . . this *person* does not deserve to own this poor horse and I was bound and determined he was not going to ride the pitiful sick thing one more step."

"Sick?" Justin surveyed the animal, a stunning bay who looked well enough to him.

"Listen. Can you not hear it?" Lady Georgiana's blue eyes blazed with anger. "The poor creature is practically gasping for breath!"

And then Justin *did* hear it, the shallow, but labored breathing as he peered into dark eyes dull with misery. How could he have missed what was now so obvious, now that the horse's indignant defender had pointed it out?

Lady Georgiana turned to her groom. "We must get him back to Ashbourne at once and apply some mustard plasters, not to mention covering him, But," she shot a look of disgust at the body lying at her feet, "what to do with this . . . this . . ."

"That is Mr. Talbot, my lady, as bought the Manor with his winnings from betting on the races. Fancies himself a gentleman and a connoisseur of the turf."

"Ha!" Georgie cast the inert figure a scornful look. "Then we shall just have to put him over the back of Bess and deliver him to the Manor on the way home, if you don't mind walking Bess and our scoundrel here."

"Not at all, my lady." Ned bent over Mr. Talbot and Justin hurried over to help him hoist Talbot onto Bess' back.

"I am happy to assist Mr. Ned, here so that you may ride ahead to Ashbourne with your patient. I assume that it will not trouble you to ride such a short distance unescorted."

Georgie gave him a sharp look. There was no missing the twinkle in his eye or the raised eyebrow. Lord, the man was even more impressive in a beautifully cut coat of dark blue that emphasized the broad chest and massive shoulders, and buckskin breeches that revealed long legs with powerful thighs, than he had been in his shirtsleeves in his forge—all in all, a man to be reckoned with, which had been her first impression, despite having mistaken him for a servant. But this man with his square jaw and proud carriage was no servant. No indeed. "Mr. Appleton, I presume." She smiled demurely.

Justin burst into laughter. Truly, Lady Georgiana Claverton was someone who was up to any challenge, "Mr. Justin Appleton of New York at your service, my lady. As I said, I shall be happy to help Mr. Ned deliver his, er, *package*."

"That won't be necessary, thank you." The response was brisk and businesslike, but not unappreciative. "We can all go to the Manor together. The more impressive escort," she directed a derisive smile at Bess' cargo, "the better. And it is on our way."

In a very short time, they arrived at the painted brick manor house which looked as though it had seen better days. "Mr. Talbot had a bit of a mishap," Ned explained to the maid who answered the door, "and his horse is very sick, so we are taking it to Ashbourne to be looked after properly. Your master will be compensated for the loss of his mount."

He slid Talbot off Bess' back and handed him over to a manservant of indeterminate age who had appeared just behind the maid, then turned away, ready to lead Bess and the sick horse, only to be interrupted by his mistress.

"Pray, miss, do you know the horse's name?"

"I . . . I believe it's Mameluke, my lady." The girl glanced nervously between Justin and Georgie before looking to the manservant for confirmation.

"Yep, Mameluke," he growled, hauling his master off into the house while the maid swiftly shut the door behind them.

"Not a very promising establishment. I would say Mameluke is well out of it," Justin remarked as they turned back towards the road. "I know, I know," he raised a hand to halt the words hovering on his companion's lips, "no one answered my door either when you called, but I have so few visitors, and Bentley is very deaf, and the maids very diligent about their own work. But the house and grounds, you must admit, are in excellent repair."

Georgie nodded, smiling. "I will give you that. Now here we are." She turned in at an impressive set of gates. "I shall just make you known to Wilson, my brother's butler, and then go to the stables to look after Mameluke."

So he ranked lower than a horse, and a sick horse at that. Justin had to admire the lady's style . . . and her priorities, but he could not help wishing, just the tiniest bit, that Lady Georgiana liked him enough to perform the introduction to her brother herself.

As it happened, no introduction was needed as just then a tall blond man with a pronounced limp came whistling around the corner of the house from the direction of a paddock just visible beyond where several superb equine specimens grazed peacefully.

"Hallo Georgie. What have we here?"

Again, Justin was entirely unsure as to whether he or the sick horse was the point of interest.

"This is your new neighbor, Mr. Justin Appleton. My brother, Lord Adrian Claverton," Georgie made the introduction. "You remember he was not at home when Ned and I went to deliver your invitation."

Justin dismounted and took the proffered hand. "I heard from one of the hired hands, however, that you had sent someone over so I thought I might take the opportunity of introducing myself."

Georgie, who had dismounted as well, had to admire the aplomb with which he delivered this complete bouncer about his *hired hand* and be grateful for it.

"Do come in, do come in and meet my wife." Adrian glanced over at Ned who was just about to lead his charges to the stable.

"It was dreadful, Adrian. The awful man was beating this poor creature who is so clearly suffering from pleurisy or influenza or bronchitis—I haven't determined what just yet—so I had to save him from that terrible person."

"Mr. Talbot, my lord," Ned supplied.

"Yes, Mr. Talbot, who, I am told, is making his money at Newmarket, so I am sure you have heard nothing good of him." Georgie turned to Justin. "My brother raises some of the fastest thoroughbreds you will ever see on the turf."

Adrian looked curiously at Justin. "I sense something missing here, Am I to assume I owe you a debt of gratitude for rescuing my sister both from her own rashness and this horse abuser? My sister is Boadicea the Warrior Queen herself when engaged in a just cause, but despite my faith in her, I cannot believe she bested a man on a horse without some help, and it goes without saying that she had left Ned in the dust miles behind her when she encountered this dastardly person."

Justin chuckled to himself. There were no flies on Lord Adrian Claverton who clearly had his sister's measure. "'Twas a mere nothing, a slight touch and the man was convinced of the rightness of her observation."

"Meaning he planted a magnificent facer and Talbot went down like a felled oak and was still insensible when Ned handed him over to his servants. Naturally," Georgie continued, frowning, "I would have gotten away on my own eventually." The frown turned into a scowl as she saw Justin struggling to keep a straight face. Then she brightened, "You and John couldn't have done better yourselves."

Justin could tell from the way she spoke that this was high praise indeed, and something tugged at his heart. How wonderful to be admired like that by a sister, and one who, up to anything herself, would expect much from others. He suddenly had the oddest craving to be regarded by her in just that sort of way.

But it was not to be. "Well, now that you two are introduced, I must go check on Mameluke." Lady Georgiana took her horse's bridle and started for the stables.

"Er," her brother stopped her, "aren't you forgetting something?"

She gave him a blank look.

"This gentleman just rescued you from a very uncomfortable situation. The least you could do is thank him."

"Oh," Georgie colored. "I am sorry, it is just that Mameluke, you see, and . . ."

"You are worried about him," Justin broke in, "I understand completely. Go take care of him Lady Georgiana."

She gave him a grateful smile and hurried off.

CHAPTER 4

"**M**Y SISTER," ADRIAN BEGAN, SHRUGGING HELPLESSLY. "Is a most redoubtable female."

"She is indeed!" He grinned. "But do come inside and meet my wife and son. Pip here," he nodded to the stable lad who had materialized at Justin's side, "will see to your horse."

Adrian led his visitor to an oak-paneled library with Palladian windows overlooking the paddock from which he had just come. A graceful fair-haired woman sat sketching by the window, a set of wooden farm animals at her feet, while a young boy romped around on a hobby horse. "Auguste," the woman looked up, "Do be careful not to knock anything over." The resignation in her voice suggested that this was not the first, nor even the second time she had uttered the words. She lifted her head as she heard footsteps, and the way her face lit up at the sight of her husband quite took Justin's breath away. Oh, he had read the poets and heard about love, but he didn't think, until this particular moment, that he had actually seen it.

"My wife, Lady Adrian." The smile Justin's host bestowed on his wife was equally tender. "May I present Mr. Justin Appleton. He heard that we tried to send him an invitation, so he came to call on us."

"Welcome to Cambridgeshire," Juliette put down her sketchbook and rose to give Justin her hand and a friendly smile. "We are glad to have you among us."

The boy galloped up to his mother's side. "Auguste!" She held out a restraining hand, "This is Mr. Justin Appleton."

The boy favored Justin with a big smile and held out his hobby horse. "And this is Prince."

"Ahem," his mother interrupted.

"Oh," Auguste bowed. "A pleasure to meet you, sir."

His mother beamed and he beamed back before continuing, "My Aunt Georgie gave him to me and she is going to buy me a real horse, not a pony, because she knows I am a big boy and I am going to learn to ride a horse, not a pony."

Justin could not help chuckling at the expression on Auguste's father's face. "Once again, I say, a most redoubtable female."

There was a long-suffering sigh. "But *this* time my sister will be responsible for the havoc she has wrought, and *she* will be the one to give Auguste riding lessons." Adrian smiled and patted his son's shoulder, leaving Justin to wonder what other sorts of havoc Lady Georgiana had wrought.

The arrival of a footman bearing a heavily laden tea tray, and the nursemaid to take Auguste off for a bath and a nap interrupted this train of thought, and they sat down to discuss other matters.

"Do tell us how we come to be neighbors," Juliette invited, taking a seat on the sofa in front of the tea tray and patting the seat next to her.

"Well," Justin disposed himself at the other end of the sofa, taking the teacup handed to him. "My stepfather, who was born in the United States, as was his father, learned a few months before he died that he had inherited Clinton House from a distant cousin many times removed. He was not well enough to travel, and my mother, who was English, was eager for me to visit her homeland, but she was also too frail to travel. I couldn't leave either one of them alone, so it was only after both their deaths that I was able to fulfill her wish and come to inspect the property."

"And was your mother from Cambridgeshire as well?" Juliette paused to nibble a bit of cake.

"A shadow crossed their visitor's face, so briefly that anyone less sharp-eyed and less encumbered with a complicated past than Juliette, might have missed it altogether.

"No, she was from Oxfordshire and was widowed before I was born. Her family had so disapproved of her husband that they not only did nothing to help her when her husband died, but encouraged her to go live with a cousin in America to hide what they considered to be the shame of a disastrous marriage. The cousin was a widow herself with the most meager of incomes, so my mother became a housekeeper to my stepfather who had just lost a young wife in childbirth. Eventually they married and he, having no heirs, adopted me."

"I can see from your expression that this new, adoptive father was a good man."

"He was." Justin nodded slowly, recalling all the times his Papa Appleton had taken time out of his busy days to explain things to his adopted heir. "He owned a shipping business in Albany, his ships coming up the Hudson with goods from the port of New York bound for Albany and parts west and returning downriver with furs brought by trappers and grain from farms in Ohio. It was his dream to be able to ship the goods from New York even farther west by means of a canal, a dream inspired by Mr. Robert Fulton whose acquaintance he made while Fulton was working on his steamboat on the Hudson. Fulton had caught the canal mania while working for the Duke of Bridgewater who, unfortunately, is no longer with us, for I would have dearly loved to study at his feet. However, I am hoping to meet the engineer, Mr. Thomas Telford, who is currently engaged in working on the Bridgewater and Gloucester canal which is a vast project. I have had some correspondence with Mr. Telford, and he has graciously invited me to view the canal but as he is constantly moving around to oversee his many projects, it may be a challenge to catch up with him."

Adrian recognized the light of the enthusiast in his guest's eyes. "Then you are something of an engineer yourself, are you?"

"I am not so sure I would qualify to be mentioned in the same breath as Mr. Fulton or Mr. Telford, but yes, I have taken quite an interest in the subject."

It was modestly spoken, but Adrian knew the sound of well-earned pride when he heard it. "Then I gather you have put some time into its study, as well as learning the shipping business from your father."

"In fact, I have. I was fortunate enough to receive my education at our Yale College which Mr. Eli Whitney also attended. His name may not be known here, but he is revered in our southern states for being the inventor of the cotton gin which revolutionized that industry. He has since built a factory in New Haven Connecticut, where Yale College is located, and has gone on to become a prodigious manufacturer of guns through an ingenious process of creating parts that will work in any one of his guns. He was so gracious as to allow me to learn at this factory, and my father was so gracious as to encourage me to do so, after I finished my studies at Yale, of course."

"A most remarkable story." Adrian, whose years of fighting in the Peninsula and later at Waterloo, had taught him the value of arms manufacture, was impressed. "And now you are turning that knowledge and interest to the construction of canals."

"Yes. Look what they have done for trade and industry in your country. You can only imagine what they will do for mine which is so much vaster."

If there was a hint of a challenge in that last statement, Adrian chose to ignore it. His fellow countrymen might belittle the brash demeanor of those from the other side of the Atlantic, but he could not help admiring it, if it was well deserved, as it appeared to be in this case. At any rate, it would make for a more interesting neighbor than most of them. Beside which, the gentleman had just rescued his sister from the consequences of her rash behavior which stemmed, as always, from her generous heart.

Adrian turned to his wife. "Mr. Appleton has just saved Georgie from a thrashing by Mr. Talbot. Do you know anything of the man?"

"A thrashing?" Juliette's delicate brows rose. "Gossip has it that the man did not have the best of reputations in London, but it was more as a gambler than a villain. He encourages others, especially the uninitiated, to bet great sums of money unwisely at the races and profits hugely from it—unsavory, but not necessarily criminal." Her brow wrinkled. "But how does Georgie come to know such a person?"

"He was mistreating a horse."

"Oh well then . . ."

"Which is now in our stables with her."

"Undoubtedly"

Adrian grinned. "You see how well my wife understands my sister."

"But men like Talbot are dreadful." Juliette turned to Justin. "My husband is always complaining that the mad desire to win money betting on racing is forcing everyone into using younger and younger horses in shorter and shorter races and threatening the breeding of truly great thoroughbreds."

"Which reminds me," her husband rose after glancing at the clock, "I have an appointment with Sir Charles Bunbury's breeder who is considering using Douro or Picton as studs for his brood mare Maria."

"Bunbury!" Justin was impressed.

"You know of him?"

"We Americans are not utter heathens, you know. The first racecourse in America was created over one hundred years before we obtained our independence from Great Britain, and one of our greatest racehorses was descended from the Godolphin Arabian, so yes, we are conversant with your leaders in the world of horse racing."

Adrian chuckled and held out his hand. "I like you better and better." He turned to his wife. "My dear, we must invite him to dinner very soon."

"And so, we shall." Juliette rose as her husband limped out of the room. "Will next Tuesday evening suit you, sir?"

Justin, who had risen as Adrian prepared to depart, smiled. "I shall be honored, and I look forward to it, but I must be going. I have taken up too much of your time already, unexpected as I was."

"Anna," Juliette nodded to the maid who had come to collect the tray," could you call for Pip to bring Mr. Appleton's horse around?"

"Do not trouble yourself," Justin waved a hand in the direction of the stables where Pip had led his horse upon his arrival. "I shall go fetch him myself."

"Very good, sir." Anna curtsied, but her mistress smiled to herself. *So that is where the land lies!*

CHAPTER 5

JUSTIN STOOD IN THE SHADOWS OUTSIDE THE STALL watching Lady Georgiana stroke Mameluke's nose and whisper in his ear. With every stroke, every whisper, the horse seemed to relax, and his breathing smoothed out. She bent over to check a mustard plaster on his chest, adjusting it and tsking under her breath. "Not an excellent job, but not a bad one either Georgie, my girl," she muttered to herself. "You'll do in a pinch when Mr. Tripp is unavailable." Clearly, she had applied the plaster herself, as evidenced by the pushed-up sleeves and the smudges on her habit. Lady Georgiana Claverton was turning out to be an amazing woman. With a grin, Justin pushed away from the post on which he had been leaning.

Georgie looked up. "I think he's already feeling better just being free from that awful man."

"And under the care of a remarkable woman."

She glanced at him in some surprise, the expression of a woman unused to, and uncomfortable with, compliments. "I was just doing what anyone with more than a pile of sawdust in their brainbox would do."

"I think not. I know very few men, and no women who would care enough for the welfare of a horse to interrupt their master's ride, much less risk their own safety over it."

In the dimness of the stable he could just make out the blush that rose to her cheeks. "Oh well, all's well that ends well, thanks to your timely assistance. Much as I hate to admit it, I really do appreciate your help."

He moved closer, staring down at her as she stroked Mameluke's nose. "And why do you hate to admit it?"

"Well, no one likes to think they can't handle themselves in any situation, do they?"

"I suppose not," he agreed, refraining from pointing out that it had been quite the opposite with every woman he had known, except his mother. They all seemed to revel in being helpless so they could beg for male assistance. Somehow, he thought she would not appreciate this observation.

It was time to redirect the conversation. "Those large black horses I saw in the paddock do not look like racing thoroughbreds to me, despite their being magnificent. Does your brother raise horse for things other than racing?"

A shadow crossed her face. "No. Those are veterans of Waterloo . . . like my brother."

Ah, that explained the limp. He nodded, hoping to acknowledge painful memories without exacerbating them, but Lady Georgiana was unfazed. "Yes, my brother, who was in the Life Guards, was badly wounded there. My other brother, Freddy, brought him here to recover, but thinking he would never walk again, Adrian was overcome with despair and grew weaker and weaker until Juliette, er Lady Adrian now, convinced him otherwise by bringing these wounded horses from his regiment here to recuperate. She had talked Mr. Dalton, the veterinarian with his regiment, into sending the horses to Ashbourne to give Adrian something to inspire him, and then she talked Mr. Tripp, the local veterinarian into caring for Adrian as well as for them."

"A veterinarian caring for a human patient?"

"Juliette knew that veterinarians do not have the luxury of amputating a limb to save a patient, so they do their utmost to save the limb and keep their patient mobile and alive which is what Mr. Tripp did for my brother—in addition to getting him involved in the care of those horses you saw in the paddock. He also had the farrier and blacksmith, Mr. Smith, with whom you are undoubtedly acquainted," she gave him a teasing smile, "construct a brace for my brother which enabled him to walk, and now, at last, he is able to do so quite tolerably on his own. Of course, Caesar was a great help."

"Caesar?"

"His own horse who stayed by his side during the entire battle after he was wounded and alerted Tom Sandys, Adrian's batman to his master's presence on the field, and the fact that he was alive."

"Yes," Justin nodded slowly, "I can see that the devotion of a horse like that could convince one to fight for life. But your sister-in-law's determination as well as her devotion is most extraordinary and inspiring." No wonder Lady Georgiana was something out of the ordinary, living with such intrepid and courageous people as Lord and Lady Adrian Claverton.

"Yes, it is, though not surprising, given the trials and tribulations she herself has weathered. As you may have guessed from her name, and the hint of French in her accent, her family, the Comte and Comtesse de Flournoy and her brother Auguste, barely escaped the revolution with their lives. When he was old enough, Auguste joined the Bourbon Cavalry Corps under the Comte d'Artois where he met the Prince of Orange and went to fight with him in the Peninsula. Juliette was the sole support of her parents, working for a modiste who used her dreadfully until a complaint of one of the patrons caused her to be cast out on the street where she was rescued by another patron, a kind-hearted actress, and eventually, after much . . . er . . . struggle she came to own her own establishment which is very a la mode." Georgie chuckled. "She can even make me cut a tolerable figure, though personally, I can't be bothered with such fripperies, but I do appreciate being comfortable in my attire, which she, alone among modistes, understands. Well, enough of that—a long answer to a short question about black horses in the paddock."

The self-conscious pause in the midst and the abrupt finish to Juliette de Flournoy's story made Justin suspect that there was a bit more misery and struggle to Lady's Adrian's history, and if Lady Georgiana considered it to be too painful or too shameful to relate, then it truly must be a wrenching tale, all of which made Justin look forward to learning more about the Clavertons at dinner on Tuesday, speaking of which . . ."Most inspiring. Lord and Lady Adrian are truly unusual people. I am honored by their invitation to dinner next Tuesday and very much looking forward to it."

"And you accepted?" She cocked her head, a challenging glint in her eye.

"Why yes. Is that so surprising?"

"It is, considering that you fobbed off the Squire's wife's invitation with the excuse that you were going to London that very day."

"But I was!"

Georgie scrutinized him with a look that would have made most men quake in their boots. "I do believe you are telling the truth."

"Of course, I am telling the truth. Why would I lie?"

She grinned. "I would have. Mrs. Selwyn is the most ridiculously self-important, odiously starched-up person in the neighborhood. Anyone with any self-respect would avoid her like the plague. Furthermore, I feel quite certain that what you received was not an invitation, but a summons."

"Well," he admitted, "it *did* rather feel like one, but I did not wish to be impolite, so I sent her what I thought was a very civil reply. Apparently it was not."

"Not to someone who is accustomed to thinking her wish is someone else's command. As I say, I would not have accepted."

"But I thought you British were excruciatingly polite."

"Perhaps we are, but we do know how to deliver a set-down to someone who deserves it."

"But then, you are Lady Georgiana Claverton."

She considered for a moment, then, shaking her head, she sighed. "You are right, of course, but . . ." she brightened, "you, as an American, could have claimed ignorance of the customs of the country, and . . ."

"And admitted that in America we are all heathens at best?"

She chuckled, but there was a hint of resignation in her voice. "Heathens. How I envy you. It must be great fun to be a heathen."

His lips twisted into a wry smile. "Not particularly. No one pays any mind to you if you are a heathen." He could see from her expression that he had struck a chord. "Besides, heathen or not, no one wishes to upset people especially if one has come among them to learn."

"Learn?" She cocked her head.

"Yes. I am very much interested in canals and am part of a joint venture at home to build a canal across New York to join us to the West. A friend of the family said I must come to England to learn from all the canal builders here, so coming to inspect the property I inherited seemed like the perfect opportunity to do so. Go ahead," he smiled at her barely concealed curiosity, "I can see you are burning to interrogate me."

"Not interrogate, precisely," she temporized, "but I can't help but wonder if your forge has anything to do with it. I mean, one does not usually see a gentleman whacking away at an anvil, and the thing you were whacking at looked nothing like a horseshoe or a harness, or . . ."

"So, you consider me a gentleman, do you?" He raised a teasing eyebrow. "I rather thought you saw me as some great oaf of a fellow." He enjoyed seeing the color stain her cheeks. He knew how she'd looked at him; she had seen him as a man and nothing else. Rank, or station in life had had nothing to do with the way her eyes had traced his body from head to foot, how her lips had parted in shock at her own reaction. Yes, Lady Georgiana Claverton had looked at him the way a woman looks at a man in the most elemental way, and from her horrified expression then and her blush now, Justin ventured to guess it was the first time she had done so.

"Oaf? Nooooo . . .," her voice trailed off and her eyes lost their focus as she re-lived the moment when she had discovered him in his forge. Then the speculative gleam re-appeared. "But what *was* the thing you were banging away at?"

Justin looked at her. She really was interested. Odd how flattering it was. "Well, when I meet these canal builders, I want to prove to them that I am not just some *heathen* from America so I have been working on a mechanism that will keep a windlass paddle in a lock from slipping out of the worker's hands and knocking him into the canal or injuring him." She still looked puzzled. "If I can prove to them, I can solve problems, that I am knowledgeable about their world, perhaps they will take me seriously. I imagine," he smiled down at her, "you can understand wanting to be taken seriously."

Georgie felt the oddest rush of happiness as she saw the sympathy and understanding warming the compelling amber eyes that seemed to be looking into her soul and liking what they saw there. She could not help griming in return as she lifted her chin. "I certainly do. But tell me, how do you know how to figure out what you want and to work with the metal to accomplish it. It must take years of study and training."

It was his turn to feel the joy of being recognized and appreciated for what he knew and could do. Even his most engineering-minded friends, and definitely his classmates at Yale, had no conception of the multiple skills required to forge iron, and even less appreciation for someone who could do it. If anything, they looked down on this plebeian skill, but this daughter of the aristocracy seemed not only to understand that much skill was required, but to admire it as well. "Well, it did take many, many hours watching and practicing under the critical eye of Mr. Crockett, our most patient blacksmith and wheelwright whose dedication to his craft and his generosity in sharing it with me were truly a gift I can never hope to repay."

Georgie liked the simple, but earnest homage to his teacher. Here was a man who felt things deeply, as she did, a rare thing among the members of the *ton* with whom she was forced to spend much of her time. Even more intriguing, was the fact that he liked *doing* things, just as she did, rather than talking about them or ordering others to do them. "You were fortunate to have such a teacher, but," she gave him an appraising look, "I think he was also fortunate in having such a dedicated student."

A slow smile softened his somber expression. "Perhaps he was. Thank you for that, Lady Georgiana."

Georgie didn't think that men, other than her oldest brother, Freddy, blushed, but the faintest coloring along his high cheekbones told her that Mr. Appleton was moved by her words.

"Well then, I must be on my way," Justin turned abruptly to the stall where Brutus was patiently waiting, "but I look forward to seeing you Tuesday, and" he turned to stroke Mameluke's nose, "to seeing you in better health now that you are so fortunate as to be in this lady's care." He bowed, leaving Georgie struggling to disguise the onslaught of unsettling emotions with a careful examination of Mameluke's mustard plaster.

CHAPTER 6

To her chagrin, Georgie was almost, but not quite, as attracted by the American's passionate interest in canals and engineering as she was by the broad shoulders and confident air that those interests had given him, but she was mistaken in lamenting that no on in the *ton* had the same sort of passionate interest. Her brother Freddy did, for one, little as his exalted position as the son of a duke allowed him to indulge in it, and Lady Verena Carstairs did, for another. In fact, Georgie had just received an enthusiastic letter from Freddy describing a visit to Lady Verena's family estate near St. Albans on his way to his own Wrothingham Abbey. *The gardens at Carstairs Hall are not to be believed,* he wrote. *Your friend, Georgie, is an absolute genius! Not only does she have an exquisite sense of design, but she knows how to make nature bend to her will—or I should say, since she has the most amiable character imaginable—she inspires nature to join with her in her creation of that design.*

"That is promising, I do agree," Juliette remarked when Georgie read that particular passage.

"Even more promising is Freddy's invitation to Lady Verena, and her mother to visit him at Wrothingham Abbey so he may consult with her about the gardens there. He is even inviting her brother, an architect who was most interested in the sketches his sister showed him of the furniture Freddy is working on with Mr. Oakley. It does seem as though Freddy is finding congenial company at last."

Georgie would have been astounded and delighted to know just how congenial things were. Strolling around the grounds of Carstairs Hall, Freddy had turned to his companion, his usually cheerful features uncharacteristically grave. "I must thank you, Lady Verena, for sharing your most exquisite creations with me. I cannot think when I have enjoyed myself more."

"You are too kind, my lord, and I apologize for prosing on about my gardens. People tell me I do that when I am discussing my favorite topic." But despite this modest disclaimer, Freddy's companion looked highly gratified.

"Ah, but I am not being kind. I am in awe of your talent and most humbly grateful to you for allowing me to appreciate its fruits." He looked down at her, his blue eyes dark with earnestness. "People think I am a paltry fellow, a here-and-thereian who cares for nothing but cravats and snuff boxes . . . and I do, but it is because I care about beauty and the design and craftsmanship of beautiful things, the understanding and creating of what is pleasing to the eye. The rest of the world neither understands nor appreciates this, but I believe you do."

Lady Verena paused mid-stroll to look up at him equally seriously, then smiled a shy quiet smile. "I believe I do, my lord. I too find myself alone in a world that does not seem to value this . . . or care."

Freddy held out his hand. "You call me *my lord*, but mayn't we just call one another friend?"

Verena took his hand, her smile widening, "Why yes, my . . . er friend," as she allowed him to place that hand on his arm as they resumed their tour of the gardens while her mother, sitting in a chair on the terrace, plucking in desultory fashion on her embroidery, allowed herself to hope that the daughter who had loathed every moment of the marriage mart might just have won the biggest catch of the Season.

The friendship begun at Carstairs Hall blossomed later on the lawns and gardens at Wrothingham Abbey as Lady Verena poked and prodded every flower and bush and peppered the head gardener with questions about the quality of the soil, drainage, and the local weather patterns.

"She's a right clever one, my lord," Ben Burrage commented later as Verena joined her mother on the terrace and Freddy went off to inspect a new walk being laid in the rose garden, "not like those hoity-toity ladies that don't know a rose from a daisy and are more afraid of getting dirt on their gowns than a killing frost. I could see she was itching to dig in the dirt herself, just to see if what we have at Wrothingham is as good as what she has at her place. From what she says, I take it she has gardens there."

Freddy could not remember when he'd heard the taciturn Ben so loquacious. "Yes, she does, and they are lovely—natural and abundant, as though they had sprung up on their own instead of being carefully planned."

"Mayhap she can spend some time here. I would be interested in what she has to say."

"High praise from you, Ben."

"I give credit where credit is due," the gardener responded stiffly before leaving Freddy to ponder the walk and his servant's remarks.

Ben might have ended the conversation abruptly with his master, but he waxed eloquent later that evening over supper in the servants' hall. "I tell you; I have never seen his lordship so easy with a woman. He was walking and talking as though they had been friends for years. And she was just as friendly right back, not like that sour-faced, betrothed-at-birth Lady Lavinia who was always trying to set him and the rest of us to rights and making us all miserable in the process."

"I've heard Lady Georgiana call Lady Lavinia Medusa, that creature as could turn people to stone just by looking at 'em—at least that's the way her ladyship tells it," A young housemaid volunteered.

"Well, she's gone, and I say good riddance to that one." Cook gave the final word, but everyone was alerted now and watched with avid, if discreetly concealed interest as their master toured his establishment with his guest, explaining every little improvement he had made at Wrothingham Abbey, each improvement as much an effort to forestall the inevitable of its having a highly critical and exacting mistress, as it was to enhance the style and comfort of the place. Where Lady Lavinia had been scornful and impatient, Lady Verena was intrigued and eager to hear every detail involved in every decision.

"It is truly exquisite, my, er, friend. You have pulled so many centuries and so many different styles into one graceful whole that is as welcoming as it is lovely," she remarked after hearing how lightening some of the dark paneling and replacing heavy Jacobean furniture with inviting chairs and settees of Freddy's own design had transformed the library into a haven instead of the forbidding cavern it had previously been.

"Why thank you. It is such a relief to share it with someone who knows how complicated these things can be."

"I find it quite perfect."

"Except for the gardens." He grinned.

"Well," she chuckled, "I do see where some improvements might be made."

"I look forward to following your every direction."

"Good heavens, you give me far too much power, especially for one who has his own well-conceived notions of esthetics, but I do look forward to working on it in consultation with you, together."

"Together," Freddy paused, "I like that. I don't think I have ever really done anything *together* with anyone before."

"Surely your brothers or your sister . . ."

"You know Georgie. Can you see her doing *together* with anyone? A law unto herself Georgie is."

Verena laughed. "That she is."

"And Adrian is all dash and horse-mad," Freddy continued, "while John . . . he is just John, quiet, but deep, very deep, and way too much a scholar for me to keep up."

But *together* worked very well where Lady Verena was concerned, so well, in fact, that Freddy could not remember enjoying himself that much ever before. Each day he woke in happy anticipation of rambling around the grounds with Verena and Ben Burrage, digging up a plant here, planting a tree or shrub there. In fact, he enjoyed himself so much that a sort of an idea formed in his mind, an idea so astounding he wished he could talk to John about it—clever fellow that he was. However, John, clever fellow that he was, proved that he was not only clever, but omniscient when he wrote in a letter that Freddy received the next day. *I understand from Georgie that you have invited her special friend, Lady Verena Carstairs, and her mother to Wrothingham so you may consult with her about your gardens. Georgie has often spoken of her talents, and since I saw you conversing so amicably with Lady Verena at mother's musicale, I trust her visit will be a delight to you both. From the little I have spoken to her, I have received the impression she is a woman of great good sense and kindness, with a passion for beauty that matches your own, so I imagine you are dealing extremely well with one another.*

That was enough endorsement for Freddy for the idea that had been forming in his mind that he sought out Lady Verena after luncheon while her mother was napping.

She and Ben Burrage were re-positioning rigid rows of roses into a more natural and inviting arrangement. "Oh excellent, excellent! They display to much better advantage your way," she exclaimed.

Freddy fixed Ben with a significant look and nodded his head toward the house.

Stifling a grin, the gardener hightailed it to the kitchen where he informed Cook, "That's it. I think we might have a new Marchioness of Wrothingham."

"Oh, I do hope so." Cook kneaded the bread in front of her with more energy than usual. "She is very kind and most knowledgeable about the culture and uses of herbs."

Freddy had, had his idea, and he was sure it was a good one, but how to begin? "Er, Lady V . . . er,I mean, Friend, I . . ." he began, looking at the roses rather than at her.

He sounded so tentative, so different from the easygoing companion of the last few days that Verena looked up in some alarm. He did appear rather anxious. She laid an encouraging hand on his arm. "Yes, my friend; say whatever you have to say for you have nothing to fear from me."

"Well, it is just that young women have such romantical notions these days, which is quite right that they should, but future dukes cannot and, well, what I mean to say is that I quite like being with you, being together—more than with anyone else—and I would dearly like to continue with you and me here at Wrothingham. That is, I am asking you if you could be my wife. I am not a knight in shining armor declaring passionate love, but I promise to honor you, protect you, and admire you with all that I have if you do me the great honor to become my wife."

A tender smile lit up her features. He was so very earnest, so very concerned, and so very dear; if she were being completely honest with herself, she could not truly say that she had ever believed in the romantical notions to which he alluded, much less entertained them for herself, but unlike Georgie, who had her inheritance from her aunt, she could not be a burden to her family. She had to marry. Lady Verena might be the daughter of an earl, but an earl burdened by debts accumulated over generations, and her elder brother showed no inclination to marry, much less marry an heiress who would fill the Carstairs' coffers. "Thank you, dear friend. I too have treasured our time together and would be honored and delighted to have it continue to the end of our days."

There was no need to say anything to the countess as they approached her in her usual chair on the terrace. The way they leaned into one another as they strolled in leisurely fashion back from the garden, and their obvious fondness for one another showed in their looks and their voices even before they shared the news.

"Of course, I shall ask Lord Carstairs' permission at the earliest possibility," Freddy assured Verena's mother.

"Of course. But how fortunate that William arrives tomorrow so that he may make your acquaintance. Of course he is not the head of the family nor the heir, but he is male so his approval carries some weight."

And it seemed, the next day, as though Lord William approved indeed, not just of the match, but of his sister's prospective groom.

Verena and Freddy had been discussing plantings along the drive when a carriage pulled up and a tall elegant young man with dark brown hair and chiseled features descended.

"William!" Verena hurried forward. "William, may I present you to Lord Wrothingham whose furniture designs I showed you and who has been so kind as to show me all the impressive changes he has made to . . ." She broke off in mid-sentence as a deep silence seemed to settle over the two men who stared at one another as though in a daze.

William was the first to recover, favoring Freddy with a dazzling smile. "I am delighted to meet the artist who is responsible for such exquisite designs, and even more delighted to discover that the artist is as elegant in person as his designs." Merry brown eyes took in Freddy's intricately tied cravat, beautifully fitted coat, and carefully selected waistcoat.

"You are too kind." A delicate flush spread over Freddy's fair skin. "And I am honored to have my simple tastes favorably regarded by a true artist."

It was William's turn to flush, but as he was not so fair as Freddy, only his very observant sister noticed.

Freddy recollected himself with an effort. "But in addition to welcoming you to Wrothingham, I must tell you I have been so bold as to ask your sister to do me the honor of becoming my wife."

"Have you now?" William cocked a quizzical eyebrow at Verena. "And has she agreed?"

"I have," she nodded, smiling.

"Well done, old fellow." William extended his hand. "I do get to call you *old fellow* if you are to be my brother-in-law, don't I?"

Freddy exhaled a breath he didn't even know he was holding in. "You do indeed. But please come in. Let me make you welcome in my humble abode, and please feel free to suggest any additions or corrections you might see that would improve it."

"Well," William's lips quirked as he glanced quickly at his sister before focusing back on her fiancée, "I would say that since my sister has consented to be your wife, a conservatory is in order."

"Of course! The very thing!" Freddy clapped a hand to his forehead. "Why didn't I think of it? Your sister is correct; you *are* a genius!"

"Doing it much too brown, but I do have my moments," Verena's brother admitted modestly. "However, I credit you with genius of your own, not just in your furniture designs, which are really quite exceptional, but in recognizing my sister for the rare person that she is. You are, as she has told me herself, a man of discriminating taste, but then," he favored Freddy with another dazzling smile, "she clearly has exquisite taste as well."

And so, the banter and compliments continued as they walked about the house before joining Lady Carstairs on the terrace.

Watching from the sidelines, Verena thought she had never seen her usually intense and reserved brother so animated and enthusiastic, and he seemed to have the same effect on her fiancée.

Once they had selected a location for the conservatory, and inspired by the project, William had sat up all night sketching plans. The next morning, he and Freddy leaned over his drawings, their shoulders touching, and as they turned to speak to one another, the space between them was alive with such mutual admiration, such unspoken communication that it left Verena breathless, so much so that she accosted Freddy in the library later that morning as he perused the recently delivered post.

"Freddy?"

He looked up in some surprise. Verena might call him friend, but she had never ventured to call him by his name, and there was an urgency in her voice that was utterly foreign to her.

He rose. "What is it my dear?" He scanned her face anxiously but could glean no clue.

"I know that William, naturally enough, will be here a great deal while the conservatory is being constructed, but after that, and after we are married, I should like him to live with us as much as possible when he does not have to be in London. He has always been a solitary fellow, but he seems to have found a special friend in you. If . . ." she twisted her hands together as she looked up at him with anxious eyes, "if, that is, such an arrangement meets with your approval. After all, it is your . . ."

"Verena," he captured her hands in his, his face aglow with gratitude, tears filling his eyes as he read the sympathy and understanding in hers, "I would like that very much, dearest of friends, and I will devote my life to the welfare and happiness and happiness of a woman and a wife I shall always strive to deserve." Raising her hands to his lips, he kissed them each in turn before releasing them to hold out his arm. "Now, let's go see what your brother has to say about this brilliant scheme of yours."

CHAPTER 7

FREDDY'S WAS NOT THE ONLY FACE IN THE CLAVERTON FAMILY that was aglow at the news of Freddy and Verena's engagement, but Georgie, being Georgie, was not so restrained in her joy as the principles. When she opened Verena's letter announcing her betrothal, she let out a jubilant whoop and raced to the library where Juliette was bent over her sketchbook.

"They're getting married! They're getting married! I did it!"

"Yes, she did it. Did I warn you yet to be extremely careful around my sister?" Adrian remarked to Justin that evening when the topic was broached at dinner to which Justin had arrived to find only one other guest, a tall serious blond man who bore more than a passing resemblance to Lady Georgiana and Lord Adrian.

"Lord John Claverton, rector of St. George's, Hanover Square, and also my brother, here for a little country air and an escape from a church empty of parishioners who have all returned to their country estates," Adrian had introduced him with a palpable pride that hit Justin in a way he could not quite describe. It wasn't envy or jealousy, but it was a sense of family that he had never known and never even realized he had missed until this moment.

"I love my sister, but I have to agree with my brother; she is the very devil," John shook his head despairingly at Georgie, but there was no mistaking the fondness in his eyes. "The instant she heard that Lady

Lavinia had cried off from her engagement to our brother, Freddy, she was plotting to bring her best friend and my older brother together, even organized a musical at Claverton House so she could do so."

"Now John, you *know* that was not the only . . ." Georgie paused as she realized that it would be airing a little too much dirty laundry, even for her, if she explained that the true purpose of the musicale was to introduce an eligible young man to the niece of the man who had engineered the *crying off* of Lady Lavinia from a betrothal made at birth. The introduction at the musicale was an expression of gratitude to the man who had saved the Claverton family from a lifetime of misery by threatening to expose Lady Lavinia as the perpetrator of a near fatal encounter between Juliette and a runaway carriage when Juliette had been one of the Ladies at Mrs. Gerrard's, London's most exclusive seraglio.

"Mr. Appleton, my sister tells me you are here, not only to acquaint yourself with your new estate, but to study our growing canal system," John broke in smoothly, turning the conversation to safer topics.

Georgie shot him a quick, grateful look, but not quick enough to escape Justin's notice, making him aware not only of how much she captured his attention, but how much he wanted to know the rest of what was obviously a complicated story. "We Americans see how much your canals have revolutionized commerce, and some of my former stepfather's friends and I are hoping to do the same in the United States."

"But Mr. Appleton wishes to do more than build canals; he wishes to improve the engineering for them." A conscious look stole across Georgie's face as she recalled the exact moment she had first observed Justin's engineering aspirations, but she recovered quickly. "He was telling me about it when he stopped by to see how Mameluke was doing after being rescued from that brute."

"Ah yes, I heard about the incident with Mameluke, and though I have the utmost confidence in my sister's grit and determination, I am grateful to you for insuring that we did not discover her lifeless body by the side of the road."

"It was fortunate that I happened by."

"You should have seen the facer he planted," Georgie broke in, "as I told Adrian, even you and he could not have done any better."

A pugilistic rector who seemed to be more amused than critical of his adventurous sister's exploits was quite a contrast to the sternly upright ministers of Justin's experience. He found he could quite like the man who had a humorous glint in his eyes and a knowing look on his face. Having spent much of his life among river captains and their crews, Justin was accustomed to observing closely in order to assess men quickly, and he recognized in Lord John Claverton someone else who possessed that skill.

"But tell me, do you employ a great deal of mathematics in your engineering endeavors?" John asked hopefully.

Justin chuckled. "I can tell from the way you pose the question that I am bound to disappoint you with my lackluster reply. Yes, I do use mathematics, but only of necessity. I do not delight in it as you must."

That earned a general laugh around the table. "My brother John not only delights in it, but he is also obsessed with it," Adrian remarked. 'You did well to be so circumspect in your reply."

"I was only wondering if he might make a fourth at whist," John defended himself.

"I am afraid the only card game I know is what we Americans call poker. I believe it is somewhat similar to what your British call commerce." Then seeing John's crestfallen look, he added, "I do, however, quite enjoy chess, if that is an acceptable substitute."

Juliette patted her brother-in-law's shoulder before explaining sympathetically, "Poor John has been at quite a loss for mental stimulation since my dear friend, and his fellow mathematics enthusiast, Helen Gerrard, got married and now, what with spending a good deal of her time at her husband's estate in the country, is less absorbed by obscure mathematical treatises than when she was single."

John laughed. "That is true, but I am not entirely without resources— the Analytical Society, for example, however, I would relish a good game of chess if you are up to it."

Justin grinned. "I am forewarned, I see. I will not claim to be a formidable opponent, but I promise to hold my own."

"Good, shall we say a game in two days' time at three o'clock . . . if you are not otherwise engaged, of course."

"I look forward to it." It was not so much the game he looked forward to, but the possibility of seeing Lady Georgiana again. Lady Georgiana's sprightliness was less noticeable among her family members than when she was on her own, but her quick smile, ready laugh, and occasional clever remarks continued to prove what Justin had already suspected; she was a character to be reckoned with. Justin liked that in anyone, but in a woman, it was as intriguing as it was rare.

"Poor John, he pays dearly for enjoying the peace and beauty of Ashbourne by the lack of intellectual challenge," Adrian chuckled, "but we do appreciate his sacrifice."

"Sacrifice is expected and therefore comes naturally to a man of the cloth," was his brother's quick rejoinder, and the general laughter that followed stuck with Justin as he made his way home that evening. He could not remember when he had felt so easy in company. Yes, he had always enjoyed the friends—mostly business associates—that his father had entertained, but now he saw the stark contrast between the lively Claverton family dinner and his own perfectly amiable, but rather dull repasts with his father and mother. How much had he missed because of the absence of brothers and sisters? Of course, he had visited the families of school friends, but somehow none of them had affected him quite this way. Perhaps it was because well brought-up sisters had deferred to their brothers, and younger brothers did the same to their elder ones, but nothing had compared to the freewheeling nature of the conversation in the Claverton family. Accustomed to the egalitarianism of American society, Justin had certainly not expected to discover such high spirits in the most elevated circles of the British aristocracy, and he found himself wishing that the chess game was tomorrow instead of two days hence. It would be too much to hope, of course, that Lady Georgiana felt the same way.

CHAPTER 8

IN FACT, GEORGIE WAS TOO CONCERNED ABOUT MAMELUKE'S welfare to think of much else. She was bound and determined to nurse him back, not only to health, but to strength and confidence, all on her own without having to call on the expertise of Mr. Tripp. It was not that she did not greatly admire or like the veterinarian; she did. It was not that he was not generous in sharing his time and his knowledge with her, which he did, abundantly, but she wanted to prove to herself that she had learned from him, from her brother, and from the talented retinue of grooms and stable-boys her brother employed at Ashbourne whom she plagued regularly for every scrap of knowledge she could get out of them.

With the exception of meals, Georgie spent most of her time in the stables with Ned tending to Mameluke, talking to him, checking mustard plasters, keeping him bundled and fed until his eyes began to brighten and the drooping head slowly raised to survey the other members of the equine community, which were an impressive lot, sharing his accommodations. "Now, if they will convince him that even though he is not cut out to be a racehorse, which he can clearly see from being with them, he can enjoy his days and be proud of providing a suitable ride for a lady, we shall be all set," Georgie remarked to Ned as she stroked the nose laid lovingly on her shoulder.

"I think he would be a good horse for me," a voice piped up behind her. "You *did* promise me you would give me a horse; you know."

"Hello, Auguste." Georgie turned to find her nephew behind her, his chin raised in a *won't take no for an answer* sort of way. "We shall see," she told him. "Yes, I did promise you."

"I would give you a horse, but first you must prove to him that you are the sort of human he wishes to befriend, and to do that, I suggest you begin by feeding him."

As she turned to fill a bucket of oats, she caught sight of Justin and John involved in deep discussion as they made their way to the stables in a leisurely fashion. "For two gentlemen who are obviously supposed to be keeping a supervisory eye on a lively five-year-old, you are doing a staggeringly poor job of it," she remarked, handing the bucket to her nephew.

"Now move forward slowly and put the oats in his trough, and when he is completely finished eating, you may pat his nose as I have taught you, but only after he is finished. Until then, you must stay very still and quiet so he can get used to you."

"My sister, the taskmistress." John shook his head. "She is almost as terrifying as my mother."

Georgie laughed. "If only we had been born puppies, she would have showered us with affection and never let us out of her sight, but I, for one, relished the freedom her preoccupation with her dogs gave me."

"You never saw such a tree climber in your life," John told Justin. "Even Adrian couldn't hold a candle to her."

"Pooh! How would you know? You always had your nose buried in a book."

"I saw plenty, believe me."

"He does, you know, see everything." Georgie turned to Justin. "It is rather unnerving. Sometimes I think he is omniscient."

"One has to be if one is to keep an eye on one's flock," John replied with a grin, but his dark blue eyes were deadly serious.

Here was a man, Justin thought, who took his priestly duties to heart—not the preaching the gospel and exhorting everyone to lead godly, righteous, and sober lives sort of duties, but genuinely caring for the spiritual welfare of his parishioners. He had that penetrating look of a man who saw and understood a great deal about his fellow men.

Justin had been the object of that very look during their just fin-ished chess game. Contemplating a move, he had happened to glance up to find his opponent studying his face instead of scrutinizing the chess pieces over which Justin's hand hovered, as any normal opponent would have.

Caught in the act, John had had the grace to look conscious. "Do you have any relatives in Cambridgeshire, other than the one from whom you inherited Clinton House, I mean."

"No. Why do you ask?"

"Well," he paused with just the slightest of apologetic looks, "it's just that you remind me distinctly of someone, though I cannot think of who it is at the moment. It's not just the features, but the way you hold yourself, the way you move. My brother said your mother was English. Did she have a large family?" Then, realizing that his inquisitiveness, startling resemblance or not, was perhaps a bit intrusive, he flushed. "I *do* beg your pardon. I am being rather rude, am I not?" He smiled, a charming, self-deprecating smile that made Justin like him all the more. "And usually, it is we British who accuse Americans of being brutally forthright, not the other way 'round. It's just that, even though I can't place the person at the moment, I sense that he is someone of whom I am fond so it would delight me to know that you are connected to him."

Well, that was a relief, Justin thought, finally deciding on his move. "Yes, my mother was English, daughter of a vicar in Oxfordshire, but she married someone of whom the family thoroughly disapproved, and they cut off all connection. When her husband died soon after they were married and she knew she was pregnant with me, they packed her off to live with a widowed aunt in New York to spare themselves the shame." Try as he would, Justin could not keep the bitterness out of his voice as he asked himself for the millionth time how a family, the family of a clergyman, no less, could be so lost to all feeling as to send a pregnant young widow all alone to a foreign land simply to save their good name.

"My mother never mentioned that part of her life before she came to America," he continued, "she refused to discuss it, actually. My family knowledge begins with her marriage to my stepfather who, very generously, took her on as his housekeeper when I was too young to know anything. After he married her and adopted me, I just assumed she didn't speak about the past out of consideration for my adoptive father. Now, as an adult, sometimes . . ." Justin broke off, realizing just how much he had revealed. He grinned. "I can see why your sister thinks you're omniscient; you not only observe intently, but you ask revealing questions."

"Again, I beg your pardon, but . . ." John, moving his own piece with a decisive plunk, looked up with a provocative smile very reminiscent of his sister's, "but you didn't have to answer, you know."

Justin couldn't help laughing, even though he could see he'd just lost the game as well as the interrogation. "And how am I to know that these questions sprang from your genuine interest and not simply from a desire to distract a gullible American opponent?"

"Touché. The inevitable American suspicion of the British determination to dominate in all things, but I *will* say," John surveyed the board, "you gave *almost* as good as you got. I thank you for an excellent game." He cocked his head. "I think I hear the approach of determined little feet," he held up a hand as Auguste materialized in the doorway, "little feet that must have escaped the nursemaid if my nephew's rapid breathing is any indication. What is it, Auguste?"

"Please, Uncle John, will you take me to the stables? Aunt Georgie is there with Mameluke, and she said she would come get me, but she hasn't, and Mama is busy, and Papa not here, and Bessie . . ."

"Is trying to keep up with you, Master Auguste. I *told* you not to bother your uncle, that I would take you to the stables as soon as I finished hemming that curtain." She glanced helplessly at John. "I do apologize, my lord, but . . ."

"He is incorrigible. I know. Mr. Appleton and I will take him."

Having seen his opponent's expression perk up with interest at the mention of his sister's name, John was happy to satisfy both his nephew and his guest by leading them to the stables.

When they arrived in the stables some minutes later, Justin was struck by the change in Mameluke's entire attitude. It was not just that he was steady on his feet, but his eyes were alert even as he adoringly nuzzled his savior's neck. It was a sight to take his breath away. What a fierce champion and defender, Lady Georgiana Claverton was, and what a change she had wrought in very little time. He leaned back against a post, enjoying the picture.

"Very good, Auguste," Georgie's voice broke into his thoughts, "you have been very quiet, and Mameluke has felt comfortable enough to eat his fill. You may approach him slowly. Hold out your hand and then stroke his nose gently, but firmly."

The little boy did as she said with a confidence and self-possession unusual in one so young, but Justin could see the longing in his eyes and the determination to prove himself worthy of his aunt's trust. The horse snuffled, allowing his nose to be stroked, then rubbed his cheek against the little boy's face.

Auguste was transfixed with joy. He looked at his aunt, who smiled gently, and then beckoned him to her. "That was excellently done. I am very proud of you for being so calm with him, and I think you will make Mameluke a most excellent companion." Her nephew wrapped his arms around her, burying his head in her skirts as she stroked the blond curls.

Justin was completely unprepared for the overwhelming emotions that washed over him: there was the tenderness of a bold and brave young woman towards a beloved nephew, the absolute trust of a young boy who recognized and admired his aunt's skill and knowledge, and the iron determination of both of them to do what was best for an abused and neglected horse.

Hot tears stung Justin's eyes, something that had never happened before, and he cursed himself for being a sentimental fool until, out of the corner of his eye, he caught a glimpse of Lord John Claverton swiping his cheek with a handkerchief he swiftly pocketed. The sight of a man in whom hundreds of parishioners confided their worst fears moved to tears, reassured Justin that he was not delusional, or not very, anyway.

"That's our Georgie," John broke into these reflections, his voice not quite steady, "she too skipped the pony part of learning to ride and went straight to the horse, insisting she could manage it. And she could too." A reminiscent smile tugged at his lips. "Auguste is very like her—willful, stubborn, and very aware of what he wants, but also able to exercise the self-discipline to achieve it, and he demonstrates a steady devotion to the people and the creatures he loves that is truly admirable. As I said, just like our Georgie." He cleared his throat briskly. "Forgive me, I must sound like the worst sort of malingerer."

"No . . .," Justin replied slowly, his face somber, "I think it . . . it sounds quite true to me, and I am glad that there is someone who recognizes that in both of them."

As do you, my friend, John thought, *as do you.*

Then Auguste caught up with them and reached for his uncle's hand. "I *told* Papa she would give me a horse."

"Yes, but not until you proved you were worthy of one and deserved to be allowed to take care of it. I am proud of you, Auguste. I don't think I know many people your Aunt Georgie would trust to do that."

Auguste gave a little skip and smiled up at his uncle. "But now let us go have some tea."

Justin fell behind as the two headed off. He had only meant to give them time alone together, but his tact was rewarded when a voice behind him remarked, "And high time it is too, for tea, I mean. I don't think Auguste could have contained his exuberance much longer."

Justin turned to Georgie, who, having caught up to him, strode along, swinging her bonnet and brushing wisps of blond hair out of her eyes. "You are to be commended. He was very good. I had not thought a child so young could exhibit such self-control."

She grinned up at him. "I can be a very terrifying creature, you know."

"I *do* know, and I don't doubt you for a moment."

"But there is nothing so inspiring as wanting something desperately." There was the slightest hint of wistfulness in her tone that made him long to ask her what *she* wanted desperately. But that was too bold a question even for a heathen American to ask.

CHAPTER 9

GEORGIE HAD SEEN THAT ARRESTED LOOK in Justin Appleton's eyes as though he had a serious question to ask her, and she wondered at it, but then they reached the house and were welcomed into the general conversation around a family tea with Auguste regaling his parents with every minute detail of his burgeoning friendship with Mameluke and she forgot all about it.

She might have remembered to wonder at it the next day except for a most unfortunate development. She had gone to the stables after lunch to check on Mameluke after the brief walk around the yard she had tried with him earlier. The horse was glad to see her, and Georgie was just about to reciprocate his nose rub with a pat of her own when she caught a slight movement out of the corner of her eye. It appeared to be a small leg whisking around the edge of the stall. There were plenty of stable lads at Ashbourne, but none who would not have stopped to talk to her and none who would have possessed a leg that short or that scrawny, and she was just about to go after him when Mameluke moved towards his manger where a suspicious pile of greens had suddenly appeared.

Georgie sprang into action. "No! Mameluke, no!" She lunged for the horse's bridle just as he was about to lower his head into the trough. At that same moment, Justin Appleton strolled into the stall. "Get that boy!" she shouted, pulling Mameluke away from the manger.

Justin knew a command when he heard one, and he dove for the lad who was scampering out of the stable, grabbing him by the ankle as they both fell to their knees. Hauling his quarry up by the scruff of his neck, Justin yanked the boy into the stall where Georgie was frantically securing Mameluke as far away from the manger as possible.

"Is this the lad you want?"

"Yes! Now, if you please . . . Oh, Ned! Thank goodness!"

Justin had always held a modest view of his own capabilities, but it was rather lowering to observe the relief with which Lady Georgiana greeted her groom, however, dealing with the issue at hand was more important than a blow to his self-esteem.

Georgie pointed to the boy in Justin's grip, "Ned, please take this miscreant away and question him until you find out everything you can about him and what he is doing here. Then, call the rest of the lads to give a thorough cleaning to this stall and this manger. I want every scrap of hay and . . . everything swept out and buried and then thoroughly washed down. In the meantime, I will put Mameluke in a stall as far away from this one as possible." With that, Georgie untied the horse and led him to the far end of the stables.

Justin released the boy to Ned. Do you need any assistance?"

"Best see to her ladyship." Ned cast a meaningful glance in Georgie's direction as he led the cowering boy away, demanding, "Now what are you doing here and who sent you?"

"I wasn't doing nothing . . ., at least nothing but help the way Mr. Tal . . ." the rest was lost as Ned led him off and Justin turned to follow Georgie as he wondered what the hell Talbot was up to now.

All thoughts of the nefarious Talbot, however, were wiped clean from his mind when he entered the stall Georgie had chosen to find her sobbing into Mameluke's neck.

"Geor . . . er, Lady Georgiana, whatever is . . ." He was at her side in an instant, pulling into his arms as her shoulders heaved and she struggled for breath. At last, she stilled and pulled away to look up at him with tear-drenched eyes darkened by fury.

"Who would do such a thing? Who would want to kill a horse? My horse?"

"Kill? How do you . . ."

"It was yew! That boy put yew in Mameluke's manger. Eating that is death to a horse! Why would anyone . . ." She dashed an angry hand across her wet cheeks. "Oh, I know, the boy had no idea what he was doing, but someone did. Someone told him to put those branches there."

"Talbot, I am sure of it!" She glared up at Justin. "But I paid for Mameluke! Why should he care what happens to a poor sick horse?"

"Because he is a thoroughly nasty piece of work, the sort of person who would use his whip on a lady, the sort of person who cannot bear to be bested at anything."

"Oh that," she dismissed it with a snort, "but a horse!"

Justin pulled her back into his arms, and Georgie, much to her chagrin, let him do so when she knew she should have been marching directly to Talbot's house and demanding his head on a pike. But it was so wonderful and comforting to lean against his broad, hard chest and feel the strength of his arms around her when she was shaking with anger and distress. How could anyone hurt an animal, especially one that was already weak and ill, though not so weak and ill as it had been, thanks to her ministrations.

One large hand reached up to stroke her hair so gently and reassuringly that the tears began to flow all over again. What could Georgie do, but lay her head on his shoulder and weep?

Justin held her, letting the storm sweep over her. Her sorrow tore at his heart, but at the same time, he was filled with an odd sense of awe and pride that she was allowing him to be there for her. The independent and determined Lady Georgiana Claverton, daughter of one of the most illustrious houses in England was permitting him, simple American commoner that he was, to see her in a moment of hurt and weakness, and, even more astounding, allowing him to comfort her.

At last, she looked up at him, her eyes shadowed with sorrow, but her chin squared, and her mouth set in a determined line. "He will pay for this, even if I have to take Adrian with me to make him . . ."

Justin loosened his hold, drawing a slow breath as he came back to reality, laying a finger on her lips. "He *will* pay for this, but I shall see to it."

Her lips tightened mulishly, but she let him continue. "Listen but a minute. Your brother is involved in thoroughbred racing, as is Talbot, scoundrel that he is, and, clearly, vindictive as he is. Your brother could be vulnerable to someone like Talbot who could possibly cause needless trouble, for who knows the man's connections in the world of thoroughbred racing and betting. I assume your brother sent a servant to Talbot's with payment for Mameluke and did not go himself?"

She shook her head.

"Lord Adrian went himself to pay Talbot?"

"No," she lifted her head proudly, "I sent Ned over with a draft from *my* banker."

"Your banker?" His jaw dropped.

"Yes, my banker" Realizing that weakly sobbing on the shoulder of a strong, handsome man was not the action of a woman independent enough to have a banker, Georgie stepped back out of the circle of Justin's arms, leaving him feeling oddly bereft.

It was not quite a lie because after all, her trustee *was* a banker, but what were details where one's pride was concerned, and, besides, Mr. Appleton's astonishment over a woman having a banker was so delicious. Somehow, she felt it incumbent upon her to let him know that even though, at the moment, she had become a watering pot like any other silly woman, she was *not* just any helpless woman. "My aunt left me a considerable inheritance so, as she wrote in her will, *Georgiana can live her life as she sees fit* and she left it in a trust such that even if I *do* marry, I still have my own funds solely at my disposal."

Justin couldn't help smiling at the challenging glint in her eye and the words, *even if I do marry.* This was the Lady Georgiana he knew, not that he would not treasure forever the tender moment when she had clung to him for comfort, but the change from angry to heartbroken had been unsettling, unsettling because at that moment, he had, had the most irrational urge to throw himself at her feet and beg her to let him protect her from any further sorrow for the rest of her life. "I gather, then, that you do not share the matrimonial ambitions of other young ladies of the *ton* who are devoted to the *marriage mart.*

"The *marriage mart,*" she scoffed, "an utter and complete bore. I went to London for the Season solely because my parents wanted me to. Naturally, they strive for my happiness, which, for most parents and their offspring, consists of getting a daughter suitably, and, one hopes, happily married. What more could a woman wish for?" The sarcastic tone left no doubt as to her views on the subject.

Strangely enough, it saddened Justin to think of this bold and idealistic—at least where horses were concerned—young woman spending her days alone, without a partner to encourage her in the pursuit of her dreams. At that moment, however, Justin was more concerned about the matters at hand.

He moved closer, fixing her with a steady gaze. "Lady Georgiana, you must promise me you will let me take care of Talbot. No," he raised a hand, forestalling the vehement objection hovering on her lips, "I understand your desire to have him thoroughly disposed of, and" he smiled encouragingly, "I approve of that desire wholeheartedly, but I believe his destruction should come from someone unconnected with you or your brother. There is too much risk to his racing enterprise. Please let me act in your stead. I give you my word I will deliver Talbot to the just desserts you wish upon him."

Georgie was about to snap back at yet another man who thought that a woman needed his help and guidance, but then she glanced up at him and was silenced by the earnest expression in his eyes. He really *did* want to help her, and he wasn't offering because she was a helpless woman, but because she was Lord Adrian Claverton's sister and he wanted to protect her brother and his business from the possible repercussions from the justice he was about to administer on her and Mameluke's behalf. She sighed. "Very well."

It was not a ringing endorsement of his abilities, but Justin could appreciate what it had cost her to accept his help. "Thank you for your confidence in me, Lady Georgiana. I promise I will not fail you." Lord, he sounded like some knight in a medieval tale setting out on a quest for his lady, but damn it, he *felt* like he was. He and his stepfather had never tolerated scoundrels, and he was not about to begin now. Not only had they not tolerated scoundrels, they had devoted themselves to routing them out and punishing them, no matter what it cost, and thus established the Appleton name as one to be respected, trusted, and reckoned with in the state of New York and beyond.

Georgiana watched the emotions play across his face as his lips tightened and his shoulders squared. In truth, he did look like an avenging hero. She could relax knowing that Talbot would trouble her no more. "Thank you. And I will do my part to make sure, without arousing my brother's suspicions," she grinned, "to make sure that the stables and their inhabitants are well protected."

She held out her hand to seal the agreement, but to her surprise, he lifted it and pressed it to his lips. Tingling warmth flooded her body, her knees weakened, and she was struck all over again with the strangely irresistible urge to throw herself against his chest and feel the reassurance of his arms around he as she had when she had broken into sobs over Mameluke's near brush with death. What was it about this man that made her want to cling to him and accept all of that strength that he offered?

Clasping her hand in both of his, Justin raised his head, his eyes dark with an emotion she could not read. "I may be away some time in order to accomplish what I need to, but trust me, you will always be in my thoughts, and you will know that everything I do is to rid you . . . and Mameluke of this evil man."

Then, with a quick bow, he was gone, leaving Georgie prey to her own emotions, equally as unfathomable as those darkening his eyes . . . or maybe she just did not want to examine them enough to identify them.

CHAPTER 10

JUSTIN'S FIRST ACTION UPON LEAVING GEORGIE was to seek out Ned, who he found cleaning tack, the young miscreant seated at his feet, industriously doing the same.

"Lady Georgiana?" The groom's grizzled features were a study in concern.

"Is recovered. I have promised her that I will see to the situation and make sure it is concluded to her satisfaction."

Some of the worry lines in Ned's face smoothed out as he read the determination in Justin's and heard the resolve in his voice. "Then I expect you'll be wanting to talk to young Sam Crimmins here so I will leave you to do so. Ned grabbed a stool from the corner, handed it to Justin, and took his leave.

Justin nodded his appreciation for the understanding and trust he read in the other man's eyes.

"Now, Sam," Justin sat down, laying a reassuring hand on the boy's shoulder, "you say you came here at the behest of Mr. Talbot who instructed you to put those branches in Mameluke's manger."

"Yes, sir." The boy's eyes, huge in his scrawny face, looked straight up at him, open and honest. "He told me he knew Mameluke was sick and this was something that would make him better. I didn't know it would hurt him, honest, sir, I didn't. They were just branches, green and all, not some potion or something."

Justin considered a moment. It did sound plausible, and the boy's face betrayed nothing, but genuine belief in what he had been told to do. A lad that young being ordered by someone in a position of authority would never think to question why the helpful branches shouldn't have been given to Mameluke before, or just offered to the new owner of Mameluke instead of being sneaked into his feeding trough. Talbot was cleverer than Justin had given him credit for, and Sam must be beholden to him.

"Tell me, Sam, how do you come to work for Mr. Talbot?"

"Well, sir, me Dad worked for him—until he died, that is, from being kicked by a horse. And after he died, Mr. Talbot took me on to help with odd jobs around the stables."

"And your mother?"

"Died when my sister was born, when I was just a lad."

As though you're not a lad now, Justin thought. Even accounting for an obvious lack of nourishment, the boy could be no older than eight.

"So, your father worked for Mr. Talbot when he lived in London?"

"Summat." Seeing the confusion in Justin's face, he elaborated. "See, me Dad was what they call a *tout*, a man as goes around all over the countryside and finds out what he can about all the horses racing, and he comes back and tells it to a *black leg* like Mr. Talbot who doesn't know nothing about horse, but he knows about betting and how much he can make by laying bets against *dead 'uns* –horses that can't win. That's what me Dad did and he got so famous for knowing everything about horses that he told me we were going to leave Mr. Talbot soon and live somewhere else with a much nicer rich owner who wanted him to come work for him, but then he was out looking at Lord Livermore's Pharoah in the pasture and the horse suddenly took a fit, just like that and kicked him in the head and killed him. Leastways, that's what Mr. Talbot told me when he promised I could still work for him. Soon after that, Mr. Talbot decided he could make more money living near Newmarket, and he brought me with him."

A simple enough tale, but Justin could just guess at the less savory implications of it from the little he already knew of Mr. Talbot. Quite possibly, it had not been the horse who killed Sam's father, but an angry Talbot, afraid of losing the man who was making him rich, and quite possibly the move to Newmarket had been the result of too many questions being asked in the London betting world about Mr. Crimmins' demise. It would be worth a visit to Lord Livermore, or his stables to hear their version of the story.

"Well, Sam, I imagine you are wondering what you are going to tell Mr. Talbot about the failure of your mission today, and I also imagine you are not looking forward to it."

Biting his lip, the boy gave an unhappy nod.

"But, if you were to come work for me, he will never have to know what happened."

"Work for you, sir?" Sam's face lit up at the possibility of working for someone whose bearing and dress spoke of a *real gentleman*, not just someone pretending to be one as his former master so obviously had. There was also something different about this man from all the toffs Sam had seen, something about the way he looked at you—straight-in-the-eye like—and something about the confidence with which he carried himself as though he knew what it was to be a man as well as a gentleman.

A frown crossed his face, and he began to worry his lip again. "But won't he find out that I am working for you and be mad and . . ." He shrank within himself as though already feeling Talbot's angry blows.

"You are right; there is that possibility," Justin admitted, determined to start this relationship the way he wanted it to continue—openly and honestly, "but I will be traveling about the country a good deal and you will be coming with me, and eventually, I hope, to America, so it is highly unlikely that he will be able to track you down."

"To America!" Sam was thunderstruck.

"Yes, America. Many a young man has left this country to make his fortune there. Perhaps you'll be another one. But right ow, we must get you cleaned up and fed. Do you think you can ride behind me on Brutus?"

"Cor, I am sure of it, sir! Sam rose and gave a swift salute with an eagerness that made Justin feel that, hasty decision though it was, he had made a good one.

Sam's estimation of his new employer rose even higher when he met Brutus. "Eh, he's a proper brute, ain't he?" He ran an experienced eye over the enormous bay's broad chest and powerful shoulders.

"That he is," Justin grinned, "but a well behaved one." He flung himself in the saddle and pulled the lad up behind him as though he were no more than a feather. "Come along, Brutus, let's get you and this lad something to eat, but first, we must introduce you to Jim."

"Jim?"

"Jim Harrington manages the stable and many other things in my life. In America, his father ran my father's estate so my father could devote himself to his shipping company. Jim and I grew up together and there is nothing I know that he doesn't—a sharp one, Jim, and a rare judge of men as well as horseflesh. You would do well to learn all you can from him."

There was no need to impress upon Sam the vast knowledge and capabilities of Jim Harrington. One glance at the blond giant with piercing blue eyes told Sam that this was another man to be reckoned with. Lord help him if that was the way all Americans were. There was no way a scrappy London lad would make his name in a place that grew men like Mr. Justin Appleton and Jim Harrington, but Jim welcomed him with a friendly enough smile, accompanied by a sharply appraising look, pointed to a comfortable berth in the stable and then led him to the kitchen where the most satisfactory grub Sam could remember ever having smelled was laid before him.

All in all, things were looking more promising than before his father had died. Though Sam was grateful to Mr. Talbot for saving him from a life of scavenging on the street, he could not bring himself to like, much less trust, the man. The shifty eyes and crafty smile ware warning enough; then there were the rumors of shady dealing and occasionally missing funds that no one could directly accuse Talbot of, but were well enough known that those who were forced to have interactions with Nathan Talbot trod carefully, very carefully indeed, all of which Mr. Justin Appleton seemed to suspect, judging from the look on his face when he had questioned him, and which Sam now hoped he would be able to prove. Then Sam would truly be free of Nathan Talbot.

Once the boy was fed and settled in back at the stable with tasks enough to keep him occupied, and a trusted groom to watch over him, Jim joined Justin in the snug little library which had become the center of the house for a man who did not entertain and was toiling over multiple designs for varied projects. Every available surface was littered with drawings. Leatherbound volumes of the classics that had graced the shelves of the previous owners had been pushed aside to accommodate Smeaton's *Experimental Enquiry Concerning the Natural Powers of Wind* and *Water to Turn Mills and Other Machines Depending on a Circular Motion* and other assorted scientific and engineering treatises as well as a variety of measuring and calculating devices.

As Jim entered, Justin gestured to a chair from which he swept a bunch of drawings before pulling an equal number of drawings off the chair opposite where he took a seat himself. "Well, what do you think? Will he do, or is he too much in thrall to that scoundrel to be of any use?"

I think you are safe enough on that point. Sam seems to bear no love for Talbot, but he is a realist, and he was grateful to be kept on after his father's death."

"Which I wonder if Talbot had a hand in."

Jim shot him a penetrating look. "Truly? You think he's that much a villain?"

"I am sure he's that much a villain. I saw the rage in his face as he tried to beat a member of the British aristocracy with a horse whip. Now he may have been so clueless that he could not guess she was the daughter of the Duke of Roxburgh, but he cannot have been so clueless as not to recognize quality when he saw it. Lady Georgiana may not sport the usual eye-catching fall-lalls of the ladies of the *ton*, but she rides a mount that is obviously beyond the means of any, but the wealthiest connoisseurs of horse flesh, and she bears herself with the assurance of one who has no betters in the social world. If Talbot was so incensed as to lose both his temper and his head to such a degree when she questioned him that he would beat her, think what he might do to the poor tout who made his fortune, but was planning to leave him. It is obvious from what I have seen of the horse Lady Georgiana rescued from him that Talbot knows nothing about horses which means Mr. Crimmins must have known a great deal indeed for Talbot to make his fortune. That, and Crimmins may have caught him cheating in ways less savory than hiring a tout to assess the competition."

"At any rate, I am hoping to uncover enough on Talbot to convince him to leave the country. To that end, I hope you will find out what you can around here and then join me in London to hang around Tattersall's, and wherever else you need to, to learn about Talbot and Crimmins while I pay a visit to Lord Livermore whose horse supposedly took exception to being watched by Crimmins and killed him, which is the tale Talbot told Sam."

"You do not like this fellow at all, do you?" Jim tilted his head, appraisingly, his eyes bright with speculation.

"No! I do not!"

There was a fierceness in his friend's response, however, that made Jim think the wish to rid the country of Mr. Talbot was more than a simple distaste for a shady fellow. Quite possibly, it was somehow connected to the most recent victim of Talbot's wrath. There was a warmth of admiration in Justin's voice when he spoke of Lady Georgiana Claverton that gave Jim pause. In all the years he had known Justin Appleton, he had never evinced the least interest in any woman, despite the many lures cast in his direction.

Jim smiled to himself as he nodded his approval of Justin's plan. This situation would bear some watching, and he couldn't wait for it to begin. A fine and generous man like his friend deserved someone who could appreciate him for the clever, energetic, and visionary person he was.

CHAPTER 11

WITH EXPERT CARE AND AN ABUNDANCE of both food and love, Mameluke progressed rapidly, so much so that Georgie confessed to Ned one morning as they led the stable's newest occupant around the pasture, "He is filling out nicely, especially the withers. He is actually proving to be more horse than I at first thought he was."

Ned nodded slowly. "I'm thinking you're in the right of it, my lady, but he'll never be a great sporting one."

"No," she grinned, "but sporting enough for Auguste when his other option is a pony."

"And speaking of the young rascal, I am surprised he has not joined us this morning."

"His mother insists he have some sort of lesson to steady him first before he comes to us. Today I believe she is making sure of his skill at addition and subtraction."

"So young?" Ned was aghast.

"*An idle mind is the Devil's workshop*, and you know he would get into mischief if he were allowed to run roughshod around here."

"Summat like his aunt, I reckon," Ned replied with a grin of his own.

Georgie laughed. The old retainer had taken a liking to her when she was just Auguste's age, and his devoted mentorship had given her a support and a freedom she would otherwise never have known, and for which she was eternally grateful. He had also provided companionship to a girl who balked at strictures like lessons and comportment, and wearing dresses that needed to be kept clean, who had rebelled against the people like her nurse and governess who were constantly admonishing her to be more ladylike. If she could have, Georgie would have lived the life her brothers did—well, Freddy, not so much, with his love of beautiful things, but John and Adrian who climbed trees and wrestled one another with abandon, ruining countless shirts and pantaloons in the process with never a thought or consequence. To be sure, being kindly sorts, they allowed her to tag along, up until the point when things got really interesting, when they would suddenly recall their brotherly responsibilities and send her home, *for your own good*. If her mother had been around more, Georgie might have reveled in her company, for she admired her mother's energy and intelligence, but the Duchess of Roxburgh was a busy woman who took her position and her duties as the wife of a politically ambitious man and the mistress of several estates seriously, and raising her spaniels even more so. So Georgie was left to make friends with the inhabitants of the stables, beginning with the horses and graduating to the stable boys, grooms, and Ned who ruled over them all with an iron fist.

From the start, she had sensed a particular friend in the groom whose face lit up whenever she appeared, and who was never too busy to let her help him with whatever task he had in hand. Being trusted to assist in grownup chores had made Georgie feel clever and special, the opposite of the way she felt with nursemaids and Miss Trimmer, the governess, who never lost the opportunity of despairing together over the likelihood of her ever becoming a true lady.

Unlike the others, Ned saw the true Georgie, accepted her, and appreciated her for who she was. Stern taskmaster that he was, he never allowed her to put less than her best effort into anything, but he let her know when she did well, and he protected her, covering up her dress with an old shirt of his, cleaning her face and hands, and smoothing her hair so that she returned to the house in roughly the same condition in which she had left.

Eventually, her father, sensing the fierce devotion Ned felt for his daughter, had assigned him to her alone and their friendship had grown and deepened, but it was not like the school and army friendships of John and Adrian; Georgie had always felt somewhat alone in the world –as she sensed her brother Freddy did as well. Then Georgie had met Lady Verena Carstairs at the select establishment for young ladies where Georgie had been sent when Miss Trimmer had washed her hands of her.

It was not that Georgie was a poor student; it was that Miss Trimmer's insistence on painting, needlework, watercolors, and music had been uninspiring in the extreme, and Georgie, bored to tears by it all, had begged for a chance to learn some of the history, natural history and the classical literature that her brothers complained of. Thus, it was that she and Verena, both fascinated with natural science, history, and languages, had, at their first meeting, been drawn to the seriousness and curiosity of the other one and had become fast friends.

Now it was Freddy—encouraged, even maneuvered, by his sister— whose solitary existence was being enlivened by Lady Verena. In spite of the aspersions her family cast on her managing ways, Georgie was frightfully proud of herself for engineering her friend's and her brother's happiness which, after Verena's letter, Georgie now felt was assured.

However, bringing Freddy and Verena together, eminently satisfactory as it was for all concerned, now created something like a hole in Georgie's life. She had relied on Verena's companionship to carry her through what Georgie considered to be the vast wasteland of the London Season. Now she would not even have that support to look forward to. To be sure, Verena would undoubtedly be in London, at Claverton House, next Season, but it would not be the same because she would be Freddy's confidante, not Georgie's. She would be on Freddy's arm, not clutching Georgie's for support and encouragement.

Georgie sighed as she walked Mameluke around the pasture. She should be happy. The horse moved smoothly and confidently without a hint of wheezing or shortness of breath. Soon, he too, would no longer need her. He would become Auguste's special friend—and that was as it should be—but suddenly the future stretched vast and empty before her, and for the first time in her life, Georgie did not know what to do. What she did know, however, was that she could not endure another Season on the marriage mart.

Unbidden, her thoughts turned to Justin Appleton. Now *there* was someone who knew what he wanted, who did not lack for exciting plans for the future. She had seen the light in his eyes and heard the enthusiasm in his voice as he spoke of his dream of connecting New York with the vast American west, using his canal and the mechanical designs which would improve the efficiency and safety of the locks along the way. How thrilling it must be to have such an impressive goal to strive for—and what did she have to look forward to? Nothing, except tolerating the least objectionable candidate her parents proposed to her as a partner. No! She was done with that! Much as Georgie loved her parents and appreciated their concern for her, she could not face it anymore. She smiled grimly to herself. At least that was some sort of goal to fight for—living her own life the way she wished. Better to live buried at Claverton than suffer through endless boring conversations with uninspiring suitors who were far more interested in her heritage, her connections, and her dowry than they were in Georgiana . . . unlike Justin Appleton.

Justin Appleton had not given a fig for her title or her fortune, but he *had* appreciated her concern and her bravery in fighting for a sick horse, and for what she continued to try to do for Mameluke. He had also recognized what she was hoping to accomplish for both Auguste and Mameluke, and the skill it took to teach a young and eager boy the responsibility he would need to assume in order to be able to call Mameluke his horse.

And what was Justin Appleton doing now, Georgie wondered. Was he tracking down the sordid past of a scoundrel? Indeed, at that very moment, Justin was sitting in the oak paneled library of Lord Livermore's Berkeley Square mansion. "Thank you for agreeing to see someone with whose name and connections you are entirely unfamiliar, my lord."

His lordship's florid features twisted into a sly smile. "Well, you were clever enough to precede your call with a most intriguing note. I admit to having wondered at Ben Crimmins' failure to appear at the appointed time, but I figured that, that knave Talbot had promised him more blunt when he heard about my offer. Still, I had expected more of Crimmins than to leave me hanging without so much as a by-your-leave."

"Then you didn't know he had suffered a mortal blow from one of your own horses in your own pasture?"

"No, I did not! Nor do I believe such a thing occurred anywhere near my property without my hearing about it. Ah, I can see from your face, Mr. Appleton, that you had your own suspicions, or you would not be here, and that you would not be at all surprised to learn that it was foul play and not a horse that led to Crimmins' death. Nor am I. You seem to have taken the true measure of Talbot—a cheat and a blackguard if ever there was one."

Justin leaned forward, hands on his knees, eyes fixed intently on his lordship. "I have my general suspicions gleaned from my own encounter with the man, but if you have specifics, I beg you to share them, my lord, as it is my intention to rid this country of him if I possibly can. And since Crimmins' son, Sam, didn't mention a grave or a funeral, I assumed, as you correctly guessed, that his father was dispatched through human effort, and the evidence quickly disposed of."

It was Lord Livermore's turn to stare. "It is, eh? Then I say, more power to you, sirrah. Take care of the rascal." He reached for a decanter, poured two glasses of amber liquid, and handed on to Justin. "Rumor in the Jockey Club is that Talbot left London because people began to call into question his phenomenal success, which was always achieved by betting against a horse, not by offering odds or betting one to one. No one actually said it, but it is a great deal easier to influence a race by making a horse lose than by making one win. Mind you, there were never any accusations, and he always settled up on time, but then, no one could last in this business if they did not."

His lordship's eyes gleamed appreciatively as he leaned forward. "But now you suspect foul play. Hmmmm, wouldn't put it past him. I barely had any contact with the fellow—a shifty sort, I always thought. And then, his tout, Crimmins, did seem rather eager to leave him. It took no convincing at all, in fact, but I was so glad to have him working for me I am afraid I did not think much about it."

Jim's findings, gleaned from talk around stables in Newmarket and among the betting crowd hanging outside Tattersall's only reinforced Lord Livermore's questionable portrait of the man. Jim, however, had uncovered more than vague innuendo. A groom who had served with another groom, now departed for whereabouts unknown, reported on a clever substitution scheme hatched by Talbot who had somehow managed to secure an inferior horse who so much resembled a popular favorite that Talbot had managed to switch the horses at the last minute and win a princely sum by betting against the favorite. Objections had been raised, but the offending groom and jockey were nowhere to be found when an investigation commenced, and it was considered such bad *ton* to complain over losing a bet that nothing was pursued any further. There were also murkier allegations of interfering with feed and water to make certain horses race slower than expected, but again, there was no absolute proof—just myriads of questions from myriad sources.

"Thank you, Jim," Justin rose after listening to his friend's report, giving him a congratulatory buffet on the shoulder. "I think we have found out enough to do the trick. Now if you can see to the settling of our bill, I have one more errand to do, and then we can be on our way," which, he admitted as he looked forward to reporting on the mission to Lady Georgiana, he could not wait to do.

CHAPTER 12

JUSTIN'S ERRAND ALSO HAD TO DO WITH GEORGIE WHOM, much to his dismay, he had been missing a great deal. He had come to London on an intriguing and compelling mission which should have fully occupied his mind and challenged his skills in investigation and hypothesis, but what would have been an extremely satisfying occupation of his time in former days now seemed sadly flat. It was not that he lacked companionship; he had had Jim who had been his partner in adventure ever since he could remember, but somehow, after Georgie's stimulating company, Jim's seemed . . . well, ordinary. Being with Georgie made Justin excited to be alive, made him look forward to the next moment, the next discussion, the next teasing, and the next chance to look into her eyes and see that she understood and appreciated him as no one else had before—and yes, the next chance to hold her in his arms, feel her heartbeat against his, see the blush rise in her cheeks, to revel in the indescribable connection between them, and to know she wanted him as much as he wanted her made Justin desperate to return to Cambridgeshire.

Hell, and damnation! Now that he considered it, he realized he was a worse case than he had thought, and he could not even lessen his longing by writing to her. All Justin could do was bring Georgie something that showed she had been in his thoughts constantly, and he wasn't even sure if that would be considered as highly improper as writing to her. What a damnable coil he had gotten himself into, but he grinned as he walked back to his hotel from Hatchard's, his parcel under his arm. It might be a damnable coil, but it had been worth it, getting to know the force of nature that was Lady Georgiana Claverton.

First, however, before he could reward himself with a visit to Ashbourne, he had to finish what he had set out to accomplish.

Two days later, Justin presented himself at the Manor at an early enough hour to ensure that its occupant was at home and to disconcert him. "Mr. Talbot, please," he announced to the same manservant of indeterminate age who had helped unload the Manor's owner from Bess' back on Justin's previous visit.

Uneasily eyeing the tall, determined gentleman requesting his master, the servant shuffled his feet. "I ain't so sure he is receiving."

"Oh yes he is, my good man, and you will conduct me to him." Lord, he sounded like the worst sort of jumped-up peer that all Americans instinctively despised! Well, it couldn't be helped. He needed to see Talbot, and he needed to see him now.

The man was seated at the breakfast table surrounded by copies of the *Calendar*, *The Turf Register*, and *The Sporting Magazine*. "What is the meaning of this intrusion, sirrah?" he shouted, rising to his feet—a mistake, since the contrast between his short, scrawny stature and Justin's formidable height and breadth only put Talbot at greater disadvantage.

"The meaning of this is that I have come to make a bargain with you. I shall purchase the Manor from you and pay your passage to New York if you will quit the country and promise never to return."

"And why would I do that?" Talbot raised his jaw and thrust out his chest.

"Because if your nefarious behavior relating to numerous races becomes widely known, you will not only lose your reputation and livelihood, but you could also be prosecuted, or worse, by those whom you have cheated."

"Hah! You have no proof of such things. Being a successful bookmaker means one is always accused of cheating by those who lose their bets. Besides, no one prosecutes someone over such trifles."

"That may be as you say, but murder is a different thing altogether, and is often a great deal easier to prove."

"Murder!"

"Of Ben Crimmins who never was kicked in the head by one of Lord Livermore's horses."

The blood drained out of Talbot's choleric countenance. "That is balderdash! You have no proof."

"Possibly," Justin's face was grim, "but I have Lord Livermore's promise of assistance on this, and you are not much liked hereabouts, so I am certain to find someone who knows something, and I promise you, I *will* find proof. I always do."

There was a calm assurance about him that spoke the truth of his assertions, and Talbot glanced about nervously to make sure no one was within earshot.

"Come, Talbot," Justin pulled a paper out of his pocket, "here is a draft on my bank in New York for the amount you paid for the Manor—with a little extra thrown in. My man, Jim, will conduct you to London where Captain Kincade Webb is preparing to set sail for New York. He will not only provide you passage to America but will furnish letters from me vouching for your position as my neighbor and a former owner of considerable property in Cambridgeshire as well as a businessman who is looking for a fresh start in the New World. Now are we agreed?"

"But . . . but . . ." Talbot snatched the draft, scrutinized it carefully and suspiciously, "I will have to give it some thought, as I have made a considerable investment in my business here, and . . ."

"You will give it no further thought, as Jim, here, "Justin nodded to his enormous and formidable companion who had materialized in the doorway, "has come to help you pack and then conduct you to London in my carriage. Consider this as an escape from the hulks, transportation to Australia, or worse, and take advantage of the opportunity to start a new life, a better life, in America. I do, however, warn you that my countrymen are very jealous of their individual rights, and take even less kindly to those who would dupe them into losing than they do here. Have care, for they will certainly be closely watching a new arrival in their midst."

With that, Justin turned on his heel and strode from the room, leaving Jim to ride herd on the miscreant, with instructions not to let him out of his sight until the ship had cast off from the London docks.

Talbot was dispensed with, Justin hoped. He had utmost faith in

Jim's ability to deliver him to Captain Webb and keep an eye on him until the ship sailed, and Webb had his instructions for insuring that he was carefully watched during his first few weeks in America. Now it was time to face Lady Georgiana, a prospect infinitely more delicate and nerve-wracking than disposing of Talbot.

It should not have worried him; after all, he had accomplished what he had set out to do, what he had promised her he would do, but her opinion mattered to him—more than Justin cared to admit. Lady Georgiana was perfectly capable of managing her own affairs, not to mention, awake on every suit. Would she approve of how he had handled things?

Justin shook his head in disgust. When had he ever doubted himself? And now he was questioning every move he made. Was it something Georgie would look upon favorably? Would she scoff, as she seemed to scoff at men trying to win that approval, or, if not that, her hand in marriage? But dammit, he wasn't trying to capture a wealthy, well-connected wife; he just wanted one of the cleverest, most courageous women—people—he'd ever met, to feel about him as he felt about her, though, now he thought about it, the idea of coming home to her every night made him dizzy with desire—or, was it more than that? Was it a longing for someone who understood him, who shared his drive to challenge himself and then to meet that challenge?

No matter. It was time to banish this fruitless obsessing and put it to the test. He grabbed the package from his desk, strode to the stables, threw the saddle on Brutus, swung himself up, and headed off to Ashbourne before he could torture himself further thinking about her, wondering if she'd missed him as much as he had missed or, or if she'd felt his absence at all.

The sad fact was the Georgie *had* missed him, but Georgie, being Georgie, had filled her time with all sorts of useful and distracting projects: caring for Mameluke, starting to put him through his paces to help him become a suitable mount for a young boy—an extremely competent and determined boy, but a very young one at that—and helping Mameluke relax around the other horses in the stable. Clearly the horse had been problematic from the outset for its original owners and breeders, which explained how Talbot had acquired him, a cheap price and a showy exterior being the only requirements of a man utterly ignorant of horses, except for betting the odds against them.

Tending to Mameluke and instructing Auguste in the horse's care and feedings, as well as convincing him to hold off riding the horse too soon, did not take up nearly enough of her time and attention. Leading Mameluke around the paddock, Georgie would catch herself wondering what Justin was doing at the particular moment, or remembering the intent look that came over his face and the energy that suffused his body whenever he described his plans for his canal, and the way that energy seemed to radiate from him and infect her, an energy that contrasted sharply with the careful cultivated languor of the men of the *ton*. She missed their private conversations in Mameluke's stall and the way Justin seemed to consider her his equal, his seriousness as he shared his hopes and dreams with her. All of this let her see that he knew that she too had hopes and dreams that meant as much to her as his did to him.

Then there was that other thing, a hunger, a tension that had seized her the moment she had caught sight of him that first time—jacketless, his sweat-soaked shirt plastered to his body, revealing the planes of his broad chest, the sleeves rolled up to expose muscular forearms and strong, capable hands, the breathlessness that overcame her every time she remembered being clasped against that hard chest, encircled by those powerful arms.

The clop of hooves interrupted her as she was giving Mameluke a rubdown and a final pat. What? She turned around. It was Brutus being led into a stall by Tim, the youngest and newest stable-boy. He was here! Justin was here! She must look a mess! Georgie shook out her skirts, smoothed her hair, rubbed her face free of possible smudges with a handkerchief and cursed herself for wishing desperately that Mameluke's stall had a looking glass. *What do you care if he's here, and why in heaven's name do you care if you are presentable or not?* She fumed to herself as she gave the horse one last pat before forcing herself to saunter casually toward the house.

CHAPTER 13

Yes, Justin was at Ashbourne, eager to see Georgie as soon as possible, but even he, heathen American that he was, knew that, that sort of thing was not done. Certain questions must be addressed and approved before he could give in to his own desires; therefore, he dismounted in a dignified manner and handed Brutus' reins to the lad who had run from the stables to greet him. He then climbed the broad staircase, giving the butler ample time to open the door and welcome him.

"Good day, Wilson," Justin handed him his hat and gloves, "is Lady Adrian in?"

"That she is, sir." Wilson motioned to the hovering footman, "Go inform her ladyship that Mr. Appleton is here and would like to see her. I trust you had a pleasant time in London, sir?" The butler led him at a more leisurely pace toward the library where the footman had disappeared.

So, it was known at Ashbourne that he had been in London! Justin didn't know whether to be gratified that his absence had been noticed or concerned for the secrecy of his mission.

"Mr. Appleton, do come in and have a seat," Juliette rose to greet him, setting aside a sketchbook and several swatches of material. "I have asked Robert to bring us some refreshment. I do hope you will join me." She indicated the chair opposite. "I hear from Georgie that you had business in London. I do hope it was successful."

It was Georgie who had mentioned his absence but kept his mission safe. That was most gratifying. "Yes, thank you," Justin took the proffered chair and began to unwrap his package, "it was most successful, but now I have come to consult you on a matter of some delicacy."

Juliette's eyebrows rose as she studied the package. "I am flattered, but." her blue eyes twinkled, "I confess, more curious than flattered. I thought you Americans dispensed with our overly nice conventions."

He smiled. "In general, we do, but in this case, your approval will greatly contribute to the success of my mission." He deposited the string he had just undone in his pocket and pulled off the paper to reveal two substantial volumes which he handed to Juliette.

"*The Anatomy of the Horse*" by Mr. Stubbs, and "*Anatomy of an Horse* by Mr. Snape?"

"Well, yes I happened across them in a bookstore and thought of how much care and attention Lady Georgiana has lavished on Mameluke— not that he didn't deserve it, of course—but I thought that if she wanted to continue caring for horses, she might appreciate these books . . . if she doesn't already own them."

Juliette had detected just the slightest tint of red outlining his cheekbones as he said *happened across*. Such prevarication was not at all like the forthright Mr. Appleton . . . and then there was *I thought that if she wanted to continue caring for horses*. Her heart did a little flip flop. How very dear that was. The man truly did care for Georgie. He truly did appreciate her for who she was, and he wanted to help her be that person. How many men could be said to recognize and value a woman as a person in her own right? Juliette was all for encouraging that sort of thinking.

She favored him with an approving smile as she handed the books back. "I think that is an excellent idea, Mr. Appleton and if I were you, I would present them to her right now." One side of her mouth quirked up. "I believe you will find her in the stables. Now, be off with you. Refreshment will wait."

"Thank you," he breathed, as he rose and bowed over Juliette's hand, struggling not to rush as fast as he could toward the stables, taking his leave while Juliette smiled to herself as she reached again for her sketchbook and swatches of material.

Justin might have strolled out of the library, but once in the hall, he broke into such a brisk pace that he caught up with Georgie before she exited the stable.

"You're here!" Georgie's face burned as she realized what she'd just said. What a goose she was! She never blushed because she refused to let anyone disconcert her, but now she was as flustered as any milk-and-water miss just out of the schoolroom. "I mean, we didn't expect you so soon." And that was worse! He would think she'd been counting the days until he returned, which she had, but . . . Hell and damnation! She was acting like a fool. Then she looked up, really looked at him, and saw the eagerness in his smile and the awkward way he clutched a badly wrapped package. Hah! He was just as nervous as she was.

"I gather you were able to conclude things to your satisfaction or you wouldn't be here to see me."

He nodded. 'I think I have. Mr. Talbot and I have agreed that he would be better off in America which is too far distant for the nasty rumors surrounding him here to follow."

"America! But how did you manage that?"

She did look suitably impressed which was not only immensely reassuring, but equally immensely gratifying.

"Well, I succeeded in convincing him that if he remained here, it was quite possible for him to wind up in the hangman's noose for the death of Sam's father, something both Lord Livermore and I would personally attend to, and then, I did purchase the manor from him so he would have the wherewithal to make a fresh start in America."

"You purchased the manor?" Her jaw dropped.

"It seemed like a good idea at the moment." He gave a deprecatory shrug.

"Justin Appleton, you are the most complete hand!"

Her eyes were so warm with admiration that he wanted to pull her into his arms then and there and kiss her breathless. Instead, he settled for thrusting the ill-wrapped package at her. "Here, I bought something for you to commemorate the success of our mission."

How sweet of him to call it *our* mission. She took it from him, staring down at it in complete bewilderment. He'd bought her a present?

"Your sister-in-law gave me permission to give it to you. She assured me it is perfectly proper."

Georgie favored him with a provocative smile, "And when did you ever worry about *proper*, I wonder?"

He grinned. "Since I met someone named *Lady* Georgiana Claverton. Now open it."

She pulled back the paper, *The Anatomy of a Horse* and *The Anatomy of an Horse*!

"You know of these?"

"Of course, I know of them! I mean, yes, Mr. Tripp has spoken of them often, but for me? You bought them for me?" Her eyes filled with unshed tears.

"Well, I thought you will always be caring for horses, no matter where you are or what happens, and, who knows, one day you might become another Mr. Tripp. I like to think that you will" He smiled down at her, his amber eyes warm with encouragement, and something else that brought the flush flooding back into her cheeks.

Then she did burst into tears.

Justin stared at her in dismay, then pulled her into his arms. "My dear girl, whatever is the matter? What have I done to upset you so? I only meant to . . ."

"No, no," Georgie sobbed, "it is not a bad thing. I am not upset at you, I . . . I . . . it is just that I am so very honored you think I should have these books."

He pulled back to look at her and his hands slid to grasp her shoulders. "Of course, you should have such books! Who deserves them more than you? Who will put them to better use than you coaxing sick horses back to health and strength?"

"But I am just a girl who loves them, and I only cared for Mameluke because . . . well . . . because he needed it."

"*Just a girl!*" He snorted. "Where is Lady Georgiana Claverton and what have you done with her? She would never admit to such namby pambyness." That earned him a watery chuckle. "You not only brought that animal back to health, but you also fought for him and, quite possibly, risked your life for him."

"Oh pooh! The man only had a whip." But as she spoke, Georgie remembered Talbot's face contorted in rage and the way he had gripped the reins. She never would have dislodged him from Mameluke if Justin hadn't come along. "It was you who saved Mameluke by planting that facer. I could never have done that."

"Once again, where is Lady Georgiana and what have you done with her? Yes, I was big enough and strong enough to pry him from the saddle and give him a floorer, but you would have figured something out to rescue that horse from that man, and if you are to become another Mr. Tripp, you must stop thinking things like that, that you wouldn't have been able to do it or that you are *just a girl who loves horses.*"

His grip on her shoulders tightened, willing her to believe in herself as he believed in her. "You scoff at those who devote themselves to the marriage mart and you once said *There is nothing so inspiring as wanting something desperately,* and watching you with Mameluke showed me that saving him was something you wanted desperately. Why not do that for other Mamelukes? Why not let that be your inspiration?"

He watched as she took in his words and saw confusion turn to hope while joy brightened her eyes. He had never seen her look so beautiful. She positively glowed with the wonder at his picture of a future for her, and it took his breath away. "You *can* do it. I know you can."

And then there was nothing to do but kiss her to prove his complete faith in her and all that she could accomplish. Slowly, Justin lowered his head and pressed his lips to hers. The kiss was simply supposed to seal his belief in her, but the minute he felt those soft lips parting under his he was lost.

With a groan Justin pulled her into his arms, reveling in the softness of her breasts against his chest, the silkiness of her skin as he slid his hands up her throat to cup her face, the caress of her breath on his own skin as she sighed at his touch, and then her hands were in his hair, pulling him closer and closer as she drank him in. This was no shy young miss, but a woman who knew what she wanted, and she wanted him! He had recognized that from the moment they had met, and he sensed that she had too, but her obvious discomfort with this attraction had also told him that, that was the first time she had even been aware that such a thing as physical desire existed.

Now she knew, and Georgie, being Georgie, was not about to pretend it didn't exist or act coquettish. They both liked and trusted one another too much to play those sorts of games, but now that they knew, now that they had read the desire in one another's eyes and felt it throbbing through their veins, what were they to do?

Justin knew what he should do in the presence of an inexperienced, gently bred, high-born young lady. In spite of her bold resolve to own her own life, and his American egalitarian disregard for aristocratic lineages, he should apologize for the liberty he had taken, bow, and leave her to her horse and her books, but she sighed and tightened her arms around his neck, and he was lost.

"Aunt Georgie!" A shrill young voice echoed through the stables as little feet pounded toward Mameluke's stall.

"Oh dear." A rueful smile, and Georgie pulled away, smoothing her hair as Auguste rounded the corner.

"Oh! Mr. Appleton you are here! I am glad, as I pa . . . par . . . pur . . . particularly wanted to ask you a question. I saw your horse. He is huge! Ned said his name is Brutus and I wondered if you might let me ride on him, if I were very good. My aunt can tell you I ride Mameluke most satis . . . satisfactorily." The little boy tilted his head, assuming his most winning smile.

Justin appeared to deliberate a moment. "I am sure you could ride Brutus but think of how Mameluke would feel if he saw you riding another horse. Mameluke knows he is your horse. He would be very hurt that you abandoned him the moment a bigger horse came along. You must make him trust you, show him that you two are fast friends—a team."

Auguste considered this for a moment. "Yes, I can see what you mean. Well then, Aunt Georgie, are you ready to go riding?"

"I certainly am. You get the saddle and blanket, and I will fetch Nero." She turned to Justin, her eyes shining. *Thank you. That was brilliant*, she mouthed, and headed out of the stall.

There was nothing for it, but to take his leave and make his way home with a heart moved by her grateful smile, and his soul and body filled with an exquisite longing for this most incredible woman.

CHAPTER 14

GEORGIE LED NERO TO MAMELUKE'S STALL and helped Auguste as he struggled to drag the saddle and the blanket over to the horse and then took them from him, putting them on Mameluke herself, all the while explaining the finer points of the procedure. She had known they would be too heavy for a five-year-old to manage, even one as tall as her nephew, but she wanted the boy to be fully aware of the effort involved in riding a horse. Then she lifted him into the saddle and was taken by complete surprise at the rush of joy as his face lit up with pride. Having Nero all saddled up already was also a pretense as she fully expected to spend most of her time walking beside Auguste on Mameluke, but she wanted her nephew to feel as though they were *riding* together so she asked Tim to follow along and help her mount when she felt easy enough to ride alongside Auguste and Mameluke.

It was an elaborate charade, for what adult in their right mind would allow a five-year-old on a horse, even one as weakened and docile as Mameluke, but Georgie remembered how she had longed to prove herself on a real horse at that age and how she fumed inwardly at being treated like a baby when she was desperate to prove herself—as she had been desperate to prove herself ever since, and no one, except Ned, bless his heart, taken her seriously . . . until now.

A lump rose in her throat at the thought of the two equine anatomy books waiting for her to dive into them. Not only did Justin Appleton think her capable of understanding and absorbing the information in them, he expected her to *do* something with it. No one, not even anyone in her family, much as they put up with and occasionally, grudgingly appreciated, her managing ways, actually expected anything of her except to behave honorably and uphold the Claverton tradition of stewardship, as they all did, whether it was her father's political endeavors, Freddy's responsibility for the title and the estates, John's devotion to the church, or Adrian's defense of his country. Now that she considered it in comparison to her brothers' services to these ideals, Georgie had always felt lacking. She, too, had wanted to dedicate herself to something inspiring, something important, but what could a mere woman do other than perform good works in the surrounding countryside? She did do good works, accompanying her mother to deliver food, clothing, and medicine to the needy and the sick, encouragement and appreciation to the aged—sustenance of whatever kind was lacking, but it wasn't enough for Georgie.

Now, however, a man with his own ideals, talents, and dreams, was encouraging her to develop hers. It filled her heart and soul with gladness and made her swear solemnly to herself that she would live up to his belief in her.

In addition to her soul being filled with gladness—her face heated at the memory—she had been filled with compelling, but less high-minded sensations in relation to the man, and it wasn't her soul or even her heart that had been filled. Her body had come alive at the first touch of Justin's lips on hers, and even she, vigorous horsewoman and outdoor enthusiast that she was, had been rendered breathless by it, taken aback by the fire, the energy, the longing that burned inside her, making her crush her body against his like a wanton . . . and she didn't care! Well, she was a bit appalled at herself for being so utterly at the mercy of her own desires, she who liked to be in charge of everything, and that loss of control was rather unnerving, to say the least, but other than that, Georgie refused to apologize to herself for her unladylike behavior, or her even more unladylike thoughts. It was so wonderful to feel the hardness of his chest against hers, the strength of his thighs as she molded herself to him. After all, she never had aspired to be a delicate lady of the *ton* in the first place.

"Aunt Georgie," Auguste piped up, breaking into her thoughts, "can we go on a *real* ride? Well, I mean," he temporized, seeing her blank expression, "next time can we go somewhere instead of riding around and around the paddock?"

Lord, Georgie wondered, had she been this exhausting? No wonder her family complained of her excessive energy the way they did. "I think you need to practice some more with Ned. Remember," she blithely ignored the scowl being sent her way, "Mameluke needs to get used to all of this too. You must never forget that you are a team, you two, as Mr. Appleton so wisely pointed out." And, not for the first time, Georgie blessed Mr. Justin Appleton for being the clever, observant man that he was. She had wanted to kiss him all over again when he had deftly deflected her nephew's interest in Brutus. Oh, who was she fooling? She had just wanted to kiss Justin Appleton again, reason or no reason. No reason was more likely, for she had clearly lost her wits where the handsome, compelling American was concerned.

"Perhaps we could ride over and call on Mr. Appleton. He calls on us a great deal, it would only be polite to visit him."

Georgie smiled at the way Auguste adopted his mother's tone of voice as he delivered this frequently overheard observation. "That *does* sound like a good idea, but it's a rather long way for Mameluke's first big outing. Perhaps we could drive over there in the gig."

"And you could show me how to handle the ribbons."

Georgie sighed. She was well served for allowing herself to cater to her nephew's ambitious wishes. Adrian would be laughing his head off if he could hear his son now. "We'll see," she temporized. "Now Tim, if you will just help me up on Nero, Auguste and I will take several more turns around the paddock." Georgie was perfectly capable of using the nearby mounting block, but she wanted to boost Auguste's confidence by making him think Tim was there to assist his aunt rather than watch out over him.

Keeping up, or trying to stay ahead of a curious, adventurous child was certainly a great deal of work, and Georgie apologized in her heart to her parents for all the times she had tried their patience to its limits. Still, it was worth the subterfuge and the aggravation to see Auguste, his face alight with his accomplishment as he slowly and carefully guided Mameluke around the paddock. Helping him down some time later, she could see that despite his exhilaration he was exhausted, but he refused to let on, even though his feet dragged as he followed her slowly back towards the Hall, until they reached the gravel drive where he suddenly bounded forward, up the broad marble steps shouting, "Robert, I rode Mameluke!" as the footman opened the door. "He's my horse now and we rode 'round and 'round, and soon Aunt Georgie and I will be riding all over the countryside like Papa!"

"Very good, Master Auguste." The young footman looked suitably impressed, but it was lost on Auguste who was already on his way to the library shouting, "Mama, Mama . . ."

"Quite an accomplishment for such a little lad." The footman shut the door behind them. "And every one of us below stairs know it is all owing to you, my lady."

"Thank you, Robert." It was not raising race horses or saving souls or preparing oneself to inherit a dukedom, but it *was* something, and the genuine admiration in the footman's voice did Georgie's heart good . . . not the good that being given two anatomy books by someone who believed she had a future taking care of horses did, but that was a dangerous comparison to make, especially as the giver would soon be departing on his visit to inspect the canals that had brought him to England in the first place.

At the moment, however, that potential traveler was doing more than inspiring Georgie with anatomy books. Not content with encouraging her to pursue her dream of helping horses like Mameluke, Justin kept a weather eye out for Adrian as he rode by Ashbourne Hall on various trips to the nearby village and was fortunate enough, a few days later, to run into him as Adrian emerged from the blacksmith's where he'd been arranging for the smith and his son to make one of their regular visits to assess Adrian's horses and their shoeing needs.

"My lord, how fortunate I am to encounter you."

"It's Adrian to you," Adrian grinned, "and I thought you heathen Americans gave no obeisance to anyone, especially an Englishman with a title."

"We don't, not in America, but even *I* know enough to realize one is much more likely to succeed if one abides by the customs of the country one is in."

"A point well made, but what is it that makes you call this a fortuitous encounter?"

"Well," Justin paused, and Adrian's curiosity was piqued. What was so momentous that made this confident and forthright man appear to weigh his words so carefully? "I just wanted to mention, outside of your sister's hearing, how impressed I am with her success with Mameluke. Even Ned thinks she has done a superb job."

Oh, so we are now on first-name footing with my sister/s groom, are we? Adrian decided that this would bear some watching. Actually, now that he thought of it, he remembered his wife saying that there did seem to be an excellent understanding between his sister and the American. He also remembered something else. "My wife tells me you brought her two equine anatomy books from London. That was kind of you."

"I believe in her." The intensity of the reply surprised Adrian, but it made him like the man the better for it. Georgie deserved to be appreciated—truly appreciated—and Adrian doubted many men, if any, had the time or the fortitude to get to know his determined, managing sister.

"I think that if she were allowed to study under Mr. Tripp, she might make an excellent veterinarian herself," Justin finished in a rush. There, he had gotten it out, not as brilliantly and convincingly as he would have liked, but he'd said it, and now it was up to the fates, and Lord Adrian Claverton, to see what happened.

"You Americans *are* egalitarian, aren't you? You are not only suggesting that an aristocrat, but a woman engage in what the *ton's* sticklers would consider to be *trade*," Then seeing the anxiety in the other man's expression, he relented, adding with a smile, "as is my wife, with Maison Juliette." Adrian laid a hand on Justin's shoulder. "But I am not one of those sticklers. I have seen too much in my life to waste my time on petty and useless distinctions, so I shall entertain the notion . . . and thank you for your confidence in my sister's capabilities."

Justin heaved a sigh of relief. He hadn't made a complete mull of it, then. "After all," he cocked his head, favoring the other man with a sly grin, "it might be to your advantage having a member of the immediate family with veterinary skills in a premier racing establishment such as yours. But I interrupt your meeting with Mr. Smith. Good day." And with that, he strode off toward Brutus who had been examined by Mr. Smith's son Tim and was now waiting patiently for his master.

CHAPTER 15

THAT MISSION ACCOMPLISHED, JUSTIN WAS FREE to attend to the final details of his departure, though, in truth, there was little to be done as Jim Harrington would be looking after Clinton House, once he had seen Talbot safely on his way to New York. It was odd how after he had first arrived in Cambridgeshire Justin had been impatient to finish up his affairs at Clinton House so he could get on to his real reason for coming to England, and now he kept finding excuses to delay his departure for Gloucestershire and the canal connecting the Severn to Gloucester which was Mr. Telford's current endeavor. It was one canal project among several of Mr. Telford's, but it was the most accessible to Clinton House and, in its connection between the River Severn and a city, it had similarities to the canal Justin and his fellow investors were building which had its inception in the Hudson River in New York. While it was true that work on the canal linking New York City to the west had been going on for some time now, Justin had not been able to get away before now. He had been frustrated by the fact that he had not been able to leave America and introduce himself to Mr. Telford before work began on Justin's own canal, but he was sure that there was still much to be learned from studying someone else's canal in the middle of its construction.

It was just that Gloucester, only two days' travel from Clinton House, which had once seemed such a short distance, now, when viewed through the lens of his burgeoning friendship with the Clavertons, and

Lady Georgiana in particular, appeared a very great distance indeed. Lately, he'd been coming to realize that he looked forward every day to the possibility of encountering her on a ride or perhaps finding some sort of excuse to stop by the stables at Ashbourne. Justin would miss that extra bit of anticipation that now dawned with each day, more than he cared to admit.

He sighed as he picked up the double-curved metal object that had been lying on his desk and wrapped it in the paper and string he'd collected precisely for that purpose. Perhaps it was a good thing after all that he was leaving; that anticipation needed to be nipped in the bud before it turned into a craving. Just thinking of craving brought the blood thundering to his ears—and elsewhere—as he recalled that searing kiss in the stable, a kiss that made him long for more, so much more—but he could not have more. He didn't want more. Who was he trying to fool? He *did* want more, but it was impossible. They were from two different worlds and had two very different dreams to pursue, but even if he couldn't have Lady Georgiana, he could give her something that would remind her of him, as he would be reminded of her every time he saw a damn horse, which meant pretty much constantly.

Justin arrived at Ashbourne just at the time when he knew Lady Adrian took a break for tea, when her husband often joined her, and when he also knew Georgie was likely to be seeing to Mameluke after giving Auguste his riding lesson. By now, she would have handed the boy off to his nursemaid for his bath and she would be enjoying a few minutes alone with the horse.

First, however, he needed to bid farewell to the lord and lady of the house who had welcomed him so warmly into their home. He dismounted, handed Brutus' reins to Pip, who had seen them coming and hurried out from the stable to welcome horse and rider with a broad grin. "I shall just see to Brutus, sir, shall I?"

"Yes, thank you, Pip." And then Justin turned to see Robert waiting at the door to welcome him. It almost felt as though he were expected, but, in truth, the staff at Ashbourne were so exceptional they anticipated their duties with a degree of seriousness Justin had rarely seen. Truly, the Clavertons, even in the privacy of their domestic circle, were an admirable group of people. It was not only Georgie he would miss when he was gone.

"Mr. Justin Appleton," Robert announced, and Juliette, clearing her lap of a sketchbook and various scraps of material rose to greet him.

"I hope I do not intrude, but I was not quite certain when my preparations for departure would be complete, otherwise I would have sent a note requesting . . ."

"Oh pooh, you know we do not stand upon ceremony here. Besides, you are practically a member of the family."

Justin was completely unprepared for the painful lump her words and kind smile brought to his throat.

"But you are leaving us? So soon? Do sit down. I shall ring for tea."

"Thank you, but I cannot stay as there is still much to do, but I wanted to thank you for your kindness to me."

There was the sound of approaching footsteps, and a moment later, Adrian appeared, remarking, "I met Robert as I was coming in and he mentioned overhearing that you are leaving us?"

It was surprisingly and unexpectedly gratifying that they would even notice, much less seem to care about his departure. "Yes, well, I had always planned to go visit some of your well-known canals, and your even more well-known Mr. Telford, with whom I have had some correspondence, and he has indicated that he plans to stop in Gloucester to inspect the work there. Having gotten things here settled to my satisfaction, I must proceed with the original purpose of my visit. At the moment, on our own canal in America, we are beginning work on the part that will connect Utica to the Hudson, and I am curious about the Gloucester connection to the Severn. I understand Telford uses steam engines, Boulton and Watt, I am guessing, to pump water out, which I would dearly love to see, especially since the Gloucester and Berkeley is the broadest and deepest canal yet, though ours, because it is in our vast country will be the longest—except for one said to be in China, I believe," he finished proudly.

You Americans and your *vast* land," Adrian chuckled. "I do hope your journey is a success, and I hear tell from Georgie that you are bringing an improvement of your own that you hope will recommend you."

Adrian exchanged a quick knowing glance with his wife as he observed the faintest hint of color tinging their guest's cheekbones. Not so awake on these things as Juliette, he had needed her to point out the special partiality his usually scornful sister had developed for the

American, and vice versa. If he hadn't had proof in Justin's suggestion of having Georgie study under Mr. Tripp, this certainly confirmed it.

Directing a meaningful smile at her husband, Juliette rose and held out her hand. "You must not let us keep you as you have a long journey ahead of you but do stop by the stables to pay your respects to Georgie. She would never forgive you if you left without bidding her farewell."

"Yes, do." Adrian extended his own hand. "You would not want to be in the bad graces of someone as formidable as my sister."

Justin laughed.

"Safe journey, and we look forward to your return," his wife added.

"Thank you." A quick bow and he was out the door heading toward the stables.

"Well, I am surprised he lingered with us as long as he did," Juliette chuckled.

"You were quite correct, my dear, he certainly does seem taken with our Georgie—unusual in a man so devoted to his projects as he is."

"Just the sort to appeal to someone who is also passionately involved in hers."

"I do hope she won't be hurt when he leaves her to pursue them permanently."

Juliette smiled mistily at her husband. "We shall see. After all, it took you some time to recognize that I could love my work and you too."

He bent to plant a heartfelt kiss on her lips. "If I'd trusted you in the first place, I could have saved myself a great deal of agony."

"But," she tilted her head, a teasing smile on her lips, "you were clever enough to realize that I was in the right of it all along, and gracious enough to admit it."

"Thank God I did!" He pulled her into his arms, just as the sound of running feet echoed in the corridor."

"Papa! Not again!" Auguste planted himself in the doorway, hands on his hips and a scornful curl to his lip as he surveyed his parents.

"I'm afraid so, lad. I cannot help it; I love your mother that much."

Auguste snorted, and his parents laughed as Robert staggered in with a laden tea tray.

Glancing around as he entered the stables, Justin assured himself that the grooms and stableboys were all elsewhere employed before he made his way to Mameluke's stall.

There was no sight of Georgie, and his heart sank. Then, he heard a rustle of hay, and she rose from the crouch she had been in as she examined one of the horse's hooves.

"Oh, it's you." She straightened, brushing a stray wisp of hair from her eyes.

"I had thought Mameluke was favoring his left hind foot a bit, but nothing seems to be amiss. I shall just have to keep an eye on it over the next few days."

Not a very promising beginning, but there was nothing for it; Justin drew a deep breath and took the plunge. "I have come to take my leave of you, I am sorry to say, for I have greatly enjoyed my visits to Ashbourne."

"You're leaving?"

Now *that* was more promising! She did look a trifle taken aback at the news. 'Yes. It is time I embark on my real purpose for coming to England, which is to learn what I can from your canal construction, so I depart for Gloucestershire tomorrow."

Georgie did not like the leaden feeling in the pit of her stomach as she absorbed the news. She did not like it at all. Yes, he had always spoken about going to see canals, but they had been getting along so splendidly she had simply pushed it to the back of her mind.

"But before I went, I wanted to give you something I made that I hope you will find useful." He held out the oddly shaped package.

What could it possibly be? Georgie was intrigued. No man had ever given her anything, except flowers, and they were always delivered in such a way that it spoke more of the giver's self-importance than consideration for the recipient who scoffed at overly elaborate nosegays that appeared from dance partners she could barely recall. She pulled back the paper to reveal a sort of double brass hook—one part square-ish and rather wide, and the other part curved and facing in the opposite direction. "Oh, thank you for . . . for . . ."

Her bewilderment was so patent, Justin couldn't help smiling as he took it from her and hung the square portion over the top of the stall, then picked up the spencer she had tossed in the far corner of the stall and hung it on the rounded hook. "I thought that if you are going to be taking care of horses, wherever, you may not always find a place to hang your things, so I made something you could carry with you."

"You made this? For me? It is perfect and so very clever!"

The glow of surprise and happiness on her face was one of the greatest gifts Justin could remember receiving. For a few moments he could not trust himself to speak, and the prospect of saying goodbye to her hollowed him out in a way he could not have imagined. "Yes, er, I wanted you to know how much I care about . . . about your being able to achieve something you have been *wanting desperately,* and I am devoted to doing anything I can to help you further that, even if it is just a hook."

"*Just a hook!*" It meant the world to Georgie. Not only had he designed, but had actually made with his own hands, something just for her, a living proof that he valued and respected her for who she was. For once in her life, she didn't know what to say or do. She, always so sure of herself—in the areas where she was knowledgeable, or in those she wasn't, which she dismissed as being unimportant–was utterly at sea.

She looked up at him, loving the seriousness in the amber eyes whose warmth showed that he saw her, truly saw her, and supported her with his entire being. "I . . . I can't thank you enough for being . . . for being the best friend I have ever known." And yes, even Verena could not be called that, not having understood Georgie so well or encouraged her so much as this man. Georgie smiled at him through tears of gratitude.

"I am glad I was able to do something for such a friend as you have become," his own voice was just the slightest bit gravelly, ". . . and to give you something to remember me by."

Justin took her hand in his, ignoring the dirt and grime of horse hoof, and raised it to his lips, and then he was gone, leaving Georgie leaning against the stall staring after him.

CHAPTER 16

NOT TRUSTING HIMSELF AN INSTANT LONGER in Georgie's distract-ing company, Justin hurried out to the stable yard where Pip was waiting with Brutus. One minute more, and he would have pulled her into his arms and they both would have been lost—or, he liked to think that both of them would have been lost—in one another.

It was a lucky escape, though it didn't feel so lucky at the moment. They both had very separate lives to live and goals to pursue. Justin had never been with anyone whose company he enjoyed more, whose spirit he admired more, and, most lowering and, most inexplicable of all, whom he desired more. Until he had met Lady Georgiana Claverton, Justin had remained blissfully unaffected by any woman; his passion was all for his work, and his carnal urges remained just that, and were easily satisfied by a partner enjoying those same urges who wanted nothing more than to satisfy them.

It had been a very near thing, this passion for Lady Georgiana, but now he was on his way to Gloucestershire and, once he had learned all he could there, with a brief return stop at Clinton House, then London, he would return to New York where his real life's work was to begin.

He should have jumped into the carriage more eagerly than he did the next day. It was a glorious morning, and the whole world—his world of calculations, plans, designs, and building—was waiting for him, but all he felt was empty as the carriage rolled over the moat at Clinton house, then down the road past the pastures and then the gates of Ashbourne where he searched in vain to catch a glimpse of an unforgettable woman astride a magnificent black horse, riding at breakneck speed, but he was not to be so fortunate, so he gave himself up to the motion of the carriage and mentally prepared himself to meet the legendary Thomas Telford.

It was a long and tedious journey and, fighting the urge to dwell on the many special moments he had spent with Georgie, Justin did his best to distract himself by framing the questions he wished to pose to Telford and the particular aspects of canal construction he wished to observe. The only break in the tedium was a stop at the iron bridge spanning the river Ouse in Newport Pagnell which was worth the stop as he strolled around, admiring the elegant structure from every angle, sketching it as best he could.

Very late in the evening the next day, the carriage rolled into Gloucester and down Southgate Street, pulling up in front of the Bell Inn, which he knew to be Telford's inn of choice on his visits to the city. He climbed down, too tired to do much more than order supper in his chambers and hope against hope that Telford, busy man that he was, had not returned to London or gone further afield to inspect the myriad projects under his supervision.

The next morning, Justin sought out the innkeeper who was pleased to inform him that yes, Mr. Telford was still lodging with them, but he had already gone out that morning, "him being a very busy man, you know, sir, but kind, exceeding kind. I expect you'll find him along the canal by the steam engine that's doing the dredging between Stroudwater and the Cambridge Arms, which, I hear tell, is in need of a bit of tinkering."

"You seem very well informed," Justin thanked him.

"Well, 'tis hard not to be, Mr. Telford being a frank, companionable sort of man, and this being such an important project connecting our city, as it does, with London and the rest of the world by water, which allows us to move so many more goods so much more cheaply than by wagon. It was quite a walk to the Cambridge Arms, but we do have horses for hire in the stables."

"Thank you. I shall be glad to avail myself of that service after my long journey."

A short while later, Justin was riding along the canal where men were digging or working on walls or unloading stone from horse-drawn dredges, the entire place a hive of activity. A sudden belch of black smoke ahead of him signaled that not only had the steam engine been repaired, but that Telford was probably to be found nearby. He rode forward and dismounted, so enthralled by the arm of the dredging machine revolving 'round and 'round so powerfully that he forgot he had come to see anyone until a voice at his elbow inquired, "May I help you, sir?"

Justin started and turned to find an open-faced young man observing his fixation with the machine approvingly. "It is something to behold, is it not?"

"That it is," the young man replied with a grin, "but it takes a certain sort of man to appreciate its importance and value. Are you interested in steam engines, then?"

"Yes, but in truth, I have come from America to learn from your expertise and experience at building canals, and in hopes of meeting Mr. Telford. The steam engine is just a fortunate happenstance."

"America! Then you *are* the sort of man to be interested in canals and steam engines if you undertook a journey like that. And you are also in luck, as Mr. Telford is right over there, the one studying those papers." He pointed to a man with dark curly hair pointing to something on the paper to another man studying it. "I am Thomas Fletcher, resident engineer here. Welcome to England, and to our canal." He held out his hand.

"Justin Appleton." Justin took it, liking what he saw in the critical, yet knowledgeable eye the man cast over the scene. "As I understand that Mr. Telford is constantly on the move from one project to another, I expect you are the one I may end up bothering the most with my questions, such as what is that instrument there?" He pointed to another man who appeared to be peering through a telescope mounted on a wheel-like base.

"That's a theodolite, and here we are fortunate enough to have one made by Troughton himself." The pride in Fletcher's voice was unmistakable. "I gather you do not have them in America."

Justin shook his head. "No, we still do our surveying with a compass and chain. A steam dredger and a theodolite—I have not been here a quarter of an hour and already my trip has been worth my while."

Fletcher smiled. "Come, let me introduce you to Mr. Telford."

As they approached the man examining the sheaf of papers, he looked up to raise an inquiring eyebrow as he saw his resident engineer leading a stranger,

"A Mr. Justin Appleton from America here to see you, sir."

Recognition dawned, and the engineer held out his hand. 'I see you have finally made it, and I gather you chose to visit this particular canal as it connects with a tidal river with stiff currents, similar to yours in . . . in . . ."

"New York, sir. And I am impressed you remembered." Justin took the proffered hand with an inward sigh of relief. While it was true that Telford had replied to his letter, it had been brief, and Justin had not been sure whether that was because the man was busy, which he obviously was, or he didn't want to be bothered, but seeing the interest in the other man's eyes, he knew it was the former.

"I gather your canal is to be quite a bit longer than anything we can boast of here."

"Yes, but America is rather larger than your *sceptered isle*," Justin replied modestly, having already seen how others' bristles had risen at the comparison of the two countries, "and it is much less civilized, which means we have had to cut our way through a good deal of wilderness, but even that has yielded some positive effects, as one of the men invented a stump puller that, with a dozen men and a team of horses, can pull thirty to forty stumps a day, not that you need that here," he pointed to the broad green fields in the distance.

"Ah, that is a difference indeed, but I suspect that the major challenges we face are the same as yours, the least among which is engineering." Telford waved the papers in his hand. "The biggest hurdle of all is funding, and one cannot build a canal if one can't pay the workers and the contractors. These men labor all day long; they *must* be paid. Now, if you'll excuse me, I have to speak to Mr. McIntosh about these bills, but perhaps we can talk at dinner. I am at the Bell, so I dine in the adjacent tavern which used to be an apothecary before the place became an inn. I leave you in the hands of Mr. Fletcher who can, I assure you, answer any questions you might have. Until dinner, then?"

"I look forward to it, sir."

Justin spent the rest of the day following Mr. Fletcher around as he described operations, battles with contractors, the sourcing of stone, and his previous experience with Telford on the Chester and Ellesmere Canal, once again linking natural waterways to one another.

By the time he returned to the inn Justin's mind was awhirl with water depth in feeder arms, difficulties with the silting up of various portions, the frustrations of having to pause work until payment could be procured for workmen, and the constant vigilance needed in dealing with contractors, and he was famished.

As he entered the taproom, Mr. Telford rose from his seat at the table to wave him over and welcome him warmly. "Fletcher tells me that you are a knowledgeable sort with an endless store of questions."

Justin laughed. "That I am, and I learned a great deal today, as there are many similarities between your endeavor and ours, but I believe our countryside, wilderness that it is, provides some challenges yours does not. We are beginning the final, most difficult phase, from Utica to Albany, where the terrain drops over a hundred feet in about eight miles, which will require a whole series of locks, with which I am sure you have had much experience."

It only needed that to get Telford talking, and Justin sat rapt as he described his experience with one canal after another, aqueducts, and locks, ship basins, and dock construction.

"And I gather from Mr. Fletcher that you have found hydraulic cement to be the most durable material to use in locks. I am curious about that."

"Yes. Oddly enough, we had only to study the ancient Romans to learn about it," Telford confessed.

"Fascinating. And speaking of locks, I wonder if I might ask you to look at a design, I have to keep the windlass on the lock paddles from slipping." Justin pulled a paper from his pocket and slid it across the table.

Telford examined it quietly for some time, turning the design to look at it from various angles, frowning in concentration while Justin, who could not remember, in all his years at school and university, ever having cared so much what someone else thought of his work, watched in anxious silence.

At last Telford looked up. 'You are a clever fellow, are you not? Now you will just have to find someone to construct it to put it to the test."

"Oh, I have already constructed it."

"Have you now? Well, I don't doubt your workmen in America are equally as good as ours here, but . . ."

"No, I mean *I* have constructed it myself."

"Well," Telford grinned broadly, "why didn't you say so in the first place? Then you are a clever fellow indeed, and I find I quite like a fellow who does not mind sullying his hands with manual work or learning the craftsmanship to accomplish such a thing. You must come to me in London when I return and show the contraption to me. I have several other projects to visit, so I am rarely at home, but I do return to London on and off, especially for meetings of the Institute of Civil Engineers, of which I am president at the moment. I do hope you will join me at one of those meetings, though from this," he pointed to Justin's drawing, "and from your fascination with our steam engine, you appear to be more taken with mechanical than civil engineering."

Justin had to agree, and the more he considered it, the more he admitted to himself that the Erie Canal and his study of canals in England, was more to fulfill his father's vision than his, for his real interest lay with the steamships that Fulton had been working on, and his own dream was the building of steamships to cross oceans and shrink the world for merchants and adventurous travelers. The conversation then turned to more general topics, Telford wanting to know more about America and sharing tales of his travels around his own country, on which he was to embark the next day.

They parted with promises to meet up in London, and Justin retired to his chambers, his mind too full of the day's experiences to fall asleep. It had been an interesting and educational day, and he was eager to return to the site to learn more, but it was not the heady experience he had looked forward to on his voyage across the Atlantic. Examining this startling discovery in greater detail, he realized that meeting Lady Georgiana Claverton and getting to know her had somehow eclipsed this journey to the canals which he had been anticipating for so long. It was a lowering thought. Even more lowering was discovering that the life Telford lived, traveling from one giant engineering project to another, which had once seemed so exciting, now appeared . . . well . . . rather lonely. Much as he loathed admitting it as he climbed into bed at last, Justin missed the warmth, happiness and other less respectable feelings that enveloped him when he was with Georgie, and he found himself looking forward to returning, not only to her, but to the welcoming friendship of the Claverton family.

CHAPTER 17

JUSTIN WAS NOT THE ONLY ONE LOOKING FORWARD to his return to Cambridgeshire, but Lady Georgiana Claverton, accustomed to needing nothing and nobody, was not about to admit, even to herself, much less anyone else, that she felt his absence, She would have done herself in before being so weakly female as to ask Justin before he left how long he anticipated it would take to learn all that he needed to know about the Gloucester canal, but now she wished she had, not in a *when will you be back* helpless sort of way, but in a casually curious, intelligent question sort of way that would have elicited at least some clue, no matter how vague, for how long she would be missing him. And miss him, she did, blast it! Georgie tugged so furiously at a snarl in Mameluke's mane that even he, gentle creature that he was, took exception to it and gave her a reproachful look.

"I know, I know, I am being beastly. I'm sorry," she muttered, straightening and pushing her own unruly mane out of her eyes.

"You? Beastly to a horse? Never!"

Georgie whirled around to find Mr. Tripp standing at the entrance of the stall, his brown eyes twinkling. "Oh, Mr. Tripp, I didn't know you would be here today. Is something wrong with one of the horses? I hadn't heard of anything," she asked anxiously.

"No, but I gather that quite a bit was amiss with this fellow until you rescued him and began looking after him." He reached over to stroke

Mameluke's nose which the horse, recognizing a true horse lover, had thrust at him.

"My brother?" She tilted her head.

"Yes, Lord Adrian did mention it to me, but, knowing you, he just took it as a matter of course that you would do such a thing. It was another gentleman who pointed out to him that you have a real gift—a gift that should not be wasted."

"Another gentleman?" It came out as a strangled squeak. Blast! Why should she care so much and hope so much about the identity of *another gentleman*?

"Yes, a Mr. Justin Appleton—I believe I have the name correctly— who, I gather, was present at the original encounter with Talbot when you so quickly and accurately diagnosed Mameluke's condition, and then so forcefully insisted on taking over his care.

"Well," Georgie flushed as she conceded, "I wouldn't have done so if Mr. Appleton hadn't come to my rescue."

"Nonsense. I know you; you would have found some way to save him, you being what Ned calls *all bottom and all heart*."

The flush turned into a full-on blush. "Oh, that's . . . that's . . . that's very kind of him."

"Ned's as good a judge of character—both human and equine—as anyone I know, and if he agrees with Mr. Appleton and your brother, then that's all the recommendation I need."

"Recommendation?"

"Well, it's a bit unusual . . . no, it is a great deal unusual, but your brother says you've been burying yourself in books on equine anatomy, and I know Ned and the stable lads have taught you all they know, so perhaps it's time I teach you what *I* know."

"*You* teach *me*?"

Georgie felt as though all the wind had been knocked out of her body, and she knew who to thank for that. Adrian was a dear, but he would never have understood how much she longed to *do* something, to *be* something, but Justin Appleton, bless his special understanding of who and what she was, did.

The veterinarian smiled. "I wish I could tell you to go to university and become a veterinarian in your own right, but we are not that enlightened yet. Maybe someday. In the meantime, however, you could become my very able assistant."

"I could?" Georgie was quite pale from excitement at the mere thought of such a possibility, and too afraid even to hope for it. "But . . . but . . . what will people say?"

Mr. Tripp chuckled. "Forgive me for being so bold Lady Georgiana, but may I venture to guess that this is the first time in your life you have uttered those words?"

She grinned. "You know me too well. Yes, it is, but do you really mean it?" Her eyes shone with unshed tears.

His shaggy brows drew together. "And you know me too well, Lady Georgiana, to know I would never mention a thing I didn't mean or wasn't willing to see through to a successful conclusion. Now, I do actually want to look at one of your brother's horses but let us agree that you will study your books and come to me with a list of questions when I return for my next regularly scheduled visit when you will accompany me on my rounds here. Is that agreed?" He held out his hand.

"Oh yes! Thank you ever so much, you are too . . ." Georgie's voice broke, and all she could do was pump his hand in a most unladylike manner.

"Very well, then. Until my next visit." The veterinarian smiled and stepped out of the stall, leaving her to stare after him, her heart pounding and her brain awhirl.

When Georgie floated into the library sometime later, Juliette knew exactly what had transpired, for Adrian had mentioned his plan, inspired by Mr. Justin Appleton, to speak to Mr. Tripp. It did her heart good to see the glow in her sister-in-law's cheeks, the sparkle in her eyes, and the tiny smile hovering over her lips. For too long Georgie had been quiet and abstracted, devoid of what Juliette liked to call her customary bounce. It would not have been noticeable to anyone but the most acute and sympathetic observer because Lady Georgiana Claverton was determined to remain unruffled in even the most distressing of circumstances, and she would not allow anything, or anyone, to upset her equanimity—anyone that was, except Justin Appleton. Oh, she had not fallen into the dismals the moment he had left, just as she had never appeared over the moon when she was in his company, but Juliette knew. She knew what it was like to feel at one with someone, to feel that they completed you, and she saw that look in Georgie's eyes whenever they fell on the gentleman from America. And her heart had ached because how could Georgie ever find what Juliette had found, true love, and family, and her profession? America was another country, an entire ocean away, and Georgie knew no one there and nothing of the place.

Thus, it was with a sigh of relief that Juliette looked up from her own work, which once had been her only life dream, and smiled. "I gather you spoke to Mr. Tripp? I am so glad for you."

"What?" Georgie plopped down on the sofa and Annie brought in a tea tray Juliette had rung for before Georgie had appeared. "Does everyone know everything about this except me?"

Juliette laughed. "It's only fair, after all you have done to manage other people's lives, that you fall victim to the same machinations yourself. "She glanced at the maid. "Thank you, Annie. As you can see, we are in need of another cup."

"Very good, my lady."

"Now," taking the cup Annie had quickly returned with, she poured the tea, handed it to her sister-in-law, and settled back with her own cup, "tell me about it."

"It was, it is . . . can you credit it? Mr. Tripp told me to study the books," pink tinged Georgie's cheeks, "Mr. Appleton brought me, and bring him my questions when he returns here for his regular visit."

"And?" Juliette prompted.

"And, he says that it is too bad women can't attend veterinary college, but . . . he would like to train me as his assistant," Georgie finished in a rush. "I can hardly believe my good fortune."

"It is not good fortune; you have earned it. But it took someone to bring it to his attention, and I am not speaking of my husband. Much as I love him, I know Adrian is too caught up in his horses to notice such things, but someone else did, someone who must admire you a great deal. Oh, not in the usual way," she hastened to add, catching sight of the scornful curl of her sister-in law's lip, "but in a believing sort of way, the sort of way that says he has the utmost confidence in your doing so brilliantly that you will more than justify his recommendation of you."

When Juliette put it that way, Georgie reflected, it did seem rather a risk that Mr. Appleton had taken on her behalf and made it even more of a special thing that he had done for her. Tears stung her eyes. She was so very grateful, and she lifted her chin proudly. "I won't disappoint him," she vowed, more to herself than to Juliette.

"I know you won't." Juliette leaned forward to clasp her hand. 'I only wish for you that you find as much joy and fulfillment in your profession as I have. I only wish . . ." she faltered.

"You only wish what?" Georgie eyed her curiously. It was unlike Juliette to be so overcome with . . . with . . . George couldn't quite say with what, but it was certainly something.

"That he was going to be around to see how splendidly you do," Juliette finished, swallowing the lump in her throat at the thought of Mr. Appleton's eventual departure.

Georgie's chest tightened painfully. *Going to be around.* She tried always to ignore it, to put it out of her mind. What difference did it make to her where Justin Appleton was. But it did. She knew it did because he'd been gone four weeks and five and a half days. She'd missed him for every single one of these days and she loathed herself for it, but sooner or later, she was going to have to face up to the fact that he was going away forever.

CHAPTER 18

GEORGIE WAS NOT THE ONLY ONE INVOLVED in self castigation, Justin was suffering much the same sort of revelations. While he could not say, down to the day, how long he had been missing her, for he had been absorbed in all that he was observing and learning in Gloucestershire, Justin had fretted at the length of absence from Georgie and had frequently chided himself for thinking about anything else except the mission that had brought him to England—learning about their canal system—and that he was fixated on a woman was even more lowering. Once upon a time he had smiled in a most superior and dismissive fashion when his acquaintances were distracted by a pretty face or coquettish ways, considering his friends to be foolishly in thrall to their emotions or baser needs. He had always felt just the slightest bit superior to them all in his single-minded devotion to his work, and now, while he had spent most of his waking hours asking questions about construction and design, observing workers and machines in minute detail, taking notes and listening carefully to everything anyone had to say, he had to admit that in the evenings, sitting in front of the fire with a glass of port, his notes in his lap, he had spent more time gazing into that fire wondering if Mr. Tripp had spoken to Georgie, what her reaction had been and (an even more lowering thought) if she knew it had been his idea to put them together, than he did looking over his notes.

At last, he had observed and noted as much as he could and, thanking everyone who had been so generous with their knowledge and time, he climbed into his carriage and headed south, desperately trying to dismiss his eagerness to be at Ashbourne again.

As luck would have it, just as the carriage rolled by the gates to Ashbourne one afternoon several days later, Justin caught sight of three riders making their way slowly, but steadily down the drive, led by a tiny figure seated very straight on a large chestnut horse, followed by another rider, so at ease in the saddle that she seemed like nothing so much as part of the horse, and finally, a burly figure on a stodgy mount some distance behind.

Hastily he rapped on the roof, and the carriage halted. "Wait here if you please," he instructed as he opened the door, dropped the steps, and climbed down, doing his best to ignore the surge of happiness that had appeared out of nowhere.

Auguste saw the carriage first, as all Georgie's attention was fixed on her nephew. "Georgie!" Then mindful of his aunt's instructions, he did his best to remain calm in the saddle and speak mildly. "It is Mr. Appleton, and he is stopping to see us!"

Georgie did not need her nephew to tell her that. Her treacherous body and heart were already tingling with joy at the sight of the tall figure emerging from the carriage.

"Mr. Appleton, Mr. Appleton, I am riding Mameluke! Georgie said we could try going all the way down the drive and look how far we have come!" Justin was glad to notice that though the boy raised his voice enough to be heard, he did it without getting so excited as to affect his mount. Truly, he had been very well taught, but Justin would have expected nothing less from as tough-minded an instructress as Lady Georgiana Claverton. Still, the boy's enthusiastic welcome was absurdly gratifying. Would that his aunt felt the same way.

"Welcome home, Mr. Appleton." Georgie rode up to greet him serenely, grateful that she'd had thirty yards of drive to compose herself. "I trust your journey was all that you'd hoped?"

"I did learn a great deal." Justin examined her face carefully, searching for signs that she was as happy to see him as he was to see her, but there was nothing more than the casual interest shown by anyone welcoming a traveler back after a journey.

Feeling his eyes upon her, Georgie congratulated herself on

maintaining rigid self –control, for once, though inside her head a happy little voice sang *He's back! He's back!* And she could not help feeling gratified that, despite the hours of wearying travel, he had stopped immediately upon seeing them instead of continuing on—as most people would have—to the welcome comfort of his own home.

"But I am glad to be home," he concluded. Then, feeling that perhaps he had admitted too much, Justin turned to Auguste, "I am delighted to see what progress you and Mameluke have made. Your aunt must be very proud of both of you."

Auguste glanced hopefully at Georgie, who smiled and nodded. "Indeed, she is."

"And she was just telling me that if I did well on the drive today, perhaps we might do some on the road. I might even be able to ride to your house someday . . . if it isn't too far. Georgie says it's a very fine, your house that is, and it even has a moat around it like the castles of olden times."

It was nonsensical to be so gratified to learn that she had spoken of Clinton House to her nephew, especially in such glowing terms, but he was. "That is most kind of her. I should be delighted to show you around some time," he included Georgie in his reply, "and perhaps your mother as well, if you would be so kind as to visit. I shall send 'round an invitation to her directly I get home. And now," realizing how odd it must appear that a man, not even a relative of the horseback riders, returning from a considerable journey, should leap out of his carriage at the first sight of them when he was only a short distance from his final destination, he added hastily "I must be getting along to Clinton House."

If Georgie did not seem to think Justin's stopping to speak to them unusual when she mentioned it to her sister-in-law sometime later, Juliette certainly did—not so much unusual as very telling. Despite what must have been his eagerness to get home, Mr. Appleton had stopped to say hello to Georgie. He must have realized how much he missed her (as much as she seemed to have missed him), and now that Juliette saw the sparkle returned to Georgie's eyes and the color back to her cheeks, and the extra bounce to her step, she knew for certain that Mr. Justin Appleton's absence had been most strongly felt. She was so very glad, for her sister-in-law's sake, that he was back, but for how long?

The promised invitation arrived before the family sat down to dinner that evening. "Ah," Juliette waved the note at Georgie as she entered the drawing room, "Auguste will be much relieved. He was so excited at the thought of visiting a place with a real moat that he was more than usually concerned that Mr. Appleton might forget all about it in the bustle of returning home. He will be delighted when I tell him first thing tomorrow morning that he has not been forgotten, and that we are to call there tomorrow afternoon, if that is convenient for us."

Convenient was hardly the right word to describe Auguste's excitement as the carriage rolled across the bridge over the moat. "And I am told that this was originally a drawbridge, and, in case of an attack, a portcullis could be dropped from the gatehouse we are now passing through," explained Georgie, who had learned as much as she could of the history of a place that had long held an attraction for her.

"Really?" Auguste's eyes were wide with excitement, and the moment the carriage door was opened, and the steps lowered, he leapt out shouting, "Mr. Appleton, Mr. Appleton, was there really a drawbridge and a p . . . a po . . ."

"A portcullis? Yes there was. And in addition, there are arrow slits and gun ports which you can see there and there." Justin pointed to some rather odd openings in the gatehouse's massive stone walls.

"And you live here?" Auguste fell into a reverent hush as he moved closer to examine everything.

"Yes, for the moment, I am fortunate enough to do so, but my real home is across the sea in America."

Juliette watched the light of enthusiasm, almost as intense as her son's, fade from Georgie's eyes. Did the man know what he'd done to her sister-in-law? Did he even care? Then Juliette looked into Justin's face and saw the same sadness there. Her mind began to work feverishly, seeking a path to happiness, which, given the obvious obstacles, certainly seemed impossible, but Juliette had seen an impossible dream come true in her own life and she was determined to do her best to make it happen in the lives of those she cared about. If Justin Appleton meant something to Georgie, then Juliette cared about him as well as her sister-in-law.

"Ah," Georgie breathed ecstatically as Justin led them into the Great Hall, "it is just as I hoped it would be!"

"Yes, it is exactly what an ancient manor house should be, down to the priest holes and secret passages."

"Secret passages? Where? Can we see them?" Auguste begged.

Justin laughed. "There is one off the library which I shall show you, but you must be careful, as no one has gone in, in years, and it is perhaps not safe to walk in, as well as very dusty."

He led them into a smaller room lined floor-to-ceiling with elegantly bound volumes, and proceeded to the fireplace where, pressing on a piece of dark wood paneling, he slid it back to reveal a small room hidden behind.

"Oh my! May I go in, Mama?"

"You must ask Mr. Appleton." Juliette lifted an inquiring eyebrow at her host.

"Yes," Justin smiled at the boy, who was quite pale with excitement, "but go carefully and take your mother with you."

"Come, Mama." Auguste tugged Juliette into the secret closet, and Justin turned to his other guest, who was staring enraptured in front of a bay of floor-to-ceiling mullioned windows at one end of the room which overlooked the moat.

"How exquisite!" Georgie turned to him, her face aglow.

As are you. Justin barely caught himself before blurting it out.

"I could sit here all day. It is so peaceful and lovely."

"It would be my pleasure, Lady Georgiana, if you would avail yourself of this room any time you so desire, whether I am here or not." Justin looked deep into her eyes as the vision of her sitting at the desk by the windows tugged at his heart. How wonderful it would be to come home to find her sitting there, waiting for him.

Hardly knowing what he was doing, Justin reached for her hand and raised it. "I would be deeply honored," he whispered as he pressed his lips against the smooth warm skin, "if you would make this room your own." The faintest scent of rosewater rose tantalizingly, and he ached to pull her to him, to bury his face in the secret seductive hollow under her ear, and to be part of her as he wanted her to be part of this house.

But that could never be. She was Lady Georgiana Claverton, descended from generations of one of England's noblest families, and he was an upstart American who had never even known his own father. Justin dropped her hand and broke away, ostensibly to look for Auguste and his mother, now emerging from the priest hole, but really because this sudden dream was too painful to contemplate.

Georgie might have thought he turned to welcome the others, but her sister-in-law knew the truth. Carefully leading Auguste back through the priest hole, Juliette had seen the adoring expression as Justin raised Georgie's hand to his lips, quickly replaced by the bleak one as he let her hand go and turned away, and she knew what it meant. She, herself, had done the same thing when recognizing her love for Adrian, she abandoned him to protect him from her own sordid past after nursing him back to health. Unlike Justin, Juliette now knew the Clavertons were made of sterner stuff. They loved where they loved and married regardless of social stature.

Justin was not the only one affected by the scene Juliette had just witnessed. As the little group toured the rest of the house, Georgie trailed along behind in a bemused silence that was most unlike her. Even during the ride home, Auguste was forced to question her twice as to whether or not she had seen the suit of armor in the long hallway before she replied, almost curtly, that she had, before falling back into a fit of abstraction.

By the time they reached Ashbourne again, Juliette had already worked out a plan to get Justin alone so she could tell him what she knew from experience about Clavertons who fell in love.

CHAPTER 19

THE VERY NEXT DAY JUSTIN RECEIVED A NOTE from Lady Adrian thanking him for being so kind as to give her son, his mother, and his aunt a tour of his fascinating house, and hoping that, as Auguste was most eager to demonstrate how much his horsemanship had improved while Mr. Appleton was away, Mr. Appleton might come to visit them that very afternoon if it were convenient or him. The final sentence instructed him, in the nicest possible way, to call upon Lady Adrian first in the library before proceeding to the stables where Auguste and Mameluke would be waiting.

The last phrase caught his eye. It was most graciously worded, but Justin knew a command when he read one, and was immediately intrigued—then concerned. Had she seen him holding Georgie's hand? Was she seizing the chance to warn him away from her sister-in-law and the damage any special interest on his part might do to her reputation? If that were the case, then it was the perfect opportunity for him to assure Lady Adrian that Lady Georgiana Claverton's success and happiness were more important to him than anything else in the world, and he would do whatever was in his power to insure that.

Juliette knew her invitation was inconveniently hasty, and she hoped Mr. Appleton didn't feel she was implying by it that he had nothing better to do than sit around and wait to be invited to Ashbourne Hall, but she knew that this was the day for Mr. Tripp's regular visit to their establishment and that meant Georgie would be safely occupied away from the house as she followed the veterinarian on his rounds.

"Ah," Juliette looked up as the footman announced Justin, "thank you for coming at such short notice. I do beg your pardon for that, but the eagerness of a young boy is hard to contain."

"I am happy to oblige and encourage such enthusiasm." Justin bowed and took the proffered seat.

His expectant posture and measuring look told Juliette everything. The man was no fool—not that she expected it from a man capable of winning Georgie's regard—so it was best to come right to the point. "I see you recognize that this was no idle invitation."

"Definitely a summons." Justin could not help smiling. His hostess' demeanor was calm and dignified, but the way she toyed with the pencil that lay next to the sketchbook she had just set aside told him that this was not going to be an easy conversation for her either.

"Ah . . . well, yes, it was, rather." She chuckled. "You see, I cannot help noticing that your friendship has come to mean a great deal to my sister-in-law, who, as you know, holds a decidedly critical view of the world, especially the male species. On top of that, you have been so kind as not only to understand her passion for horses, but to recognize her unusual affinity for them, and to actively encourage that affinity with your gift of the equine anatomy books and your suggestion that she study under Mr. Tripp, who, this being his day at Ashbourne, is instructing her as we speak. These are the actions of a man who cares a great deal about her happiness."

She raised her hand to forestall whatever protestations she could see were hovering on his lips. "Hear me out, sir. I think you may mistake my motive in broaching this subject. You see, I caught a glimpse of you and Georgie when Auguste and I emerged from the priest hole. I read the sorrow in your eyes and the resolve in the set of your jaw. You knew that no matter how much you cared for her, she was not for you, and you hoped she felt the same way she, a titled lady of an ancient noble family, and you an American who, no matter how much he might believe in equality among his fellow men (and women) respects the traditions of a country not his own."

She tilted her head, fixing him with dark blue eyes that saw entirely too much for Justin's peace of mind. "Have I guessed correctly?"

"You have," he admitted with a rueful smile, "But," he hastened to add, "I can reassure you that Lady Georgiana's happiness is everything to me, and therefore she will never know of my . . ."

Again, Juliette raised her hand, "You mistake my meaning, Mr. Appleton, I have asked you here not to discourage your suit, but to encourage it."

With a supreme effort, Justin kept his jaw from dropping, but he must not have been as successful as he hoped, for his hostess' spurt of laughter broke through his stunned silence.

"Forgive me, but your expression is indeed comical." She sobered, "Not that I blame you, but I think it is time to tell you a story—my story—to prove my point, which is that rank means nothing to my sister-in-law, and not so much to her family as you might think, where true love is involved.

"Oh?" He leaned forward, recalling the rather abrupt conclusion to Georgie's story of Lord and Lady Adrian's courtship. So there *had been* more to the tale than she had let on! He'd had the feeling that Georgie had hurried through the end bit after talking about Lady Adrian's being let go from her position at a modiste's.

"Not to put too fine a point upon it, when my husband met me, I was one of Mrs. Gerrard's ladies. Actually it was his brother, Freddy, who was visiting me, but he spied Adrian from a window and waved him in. "She saw the blank look on Justin's face. "I gather you are not familiar with Mrs. Gerrard's."

He shook his head.

"It is London's most exclusive seraglio."

Still the blank look.

"I believe you Americans would call it a brothel."

His brows rose. "Aaah."

"Ah indeed! So, you see, an American with no title cannot compare with a courtesan."

"But regardless of your situation at the time, you were a daughter of the French nobility."

She snorted. "I see that Georgie has told you some of my story, at least. I may have been the daughter of the Comte and Comtesse de Flournoy, but they did not take kindly to my working for a living at a respectable modiste's, and when I was raped by the husband of one of our patronesses—with unfortunate consequences—and was, therefore, thrown out on the street, they disowned me. Another of our patronesses, an actress, rescued me, nursed me back to health, and introduced me to Helen Gerrard who, having suffered a similar fate herself, took women like me into her house in St. James' Square, which had been left her by an appreciative and grateful lover. Determined to help others like herself, she turned it into a most exclusive establishment which charges its patrons enormous sums in exchange for charming and intelligent female companionship, and Helen made sure that everyone in her care invested their earnings wisely so as to provide for themselves in their old age or to follow their dreams, as I have done." With a proud smile she gestured toward her sketchbook. "Helen is now a countess in her own right and devotes herself to female education, while the actress who nursed me back to health now oversees Mrs. Gerrard's, but not before Helen helped another one of her *ladies* achieve her dream of becoming a celebrated opera singer. Lady Maximilian Hawkesbury, formerly Grace Owen, is now a fixture at La Scala and wife of the British Resident in Turin."

"It was Adrian's brother, Freddy, Marquess of Wrothingham, who, admiring my dress at the opera and, being something of a fashion connoisseur, begged for an introduction. It was he who made me known to Adrian and, unbeknownst to us, encouraged our acquaintance, though, I do admit that, much as I tried to ignore it, it was love at first sight."

The tenderness in her smile and the glow on her face as she spoke these words took Justin's breath away.

"So, you see, I know what you suffer. I knew I would be a mesalliance for Adrian, and I drove him away." Juliette paused a moment before regaining her voice. "But, fortunately for me, he was made of sterner stuff. He sought out my parents in France where they were mourning my brother Auguste's death at Waterloo and convinced them that their only chance of having a grandchild and the continuation of the de Flournoy line, in blood, if not in name, was to bless our marriage. And," she chuckled, "I believe they took a great deal more convincing than the Duke and Duchess of Roxburgh did because of Georgie's having helped me set up my shop and being one of my staunch supporters as well as one of my first patronesses, along with her friend Lady Verena

Carstairs. Freddy, too, praised me to the skies and made all sorts of decorative contributions to my shop, so I was already known to the family. Besides, my family, though very much poorer, had a far more ancient lineage than the Clavertons who only rose to wealth and power in the Tudor age, and they felt it was a bit of a come-down for me—despite my unfortunate history—to be marrying Lord Adrian rather than their choice, the Comte de Montmorency who, though as poor as a church mouse, not to mention that he was as weak-jawed as he was weak-willed, had more illustrious forbears than my husband."

"So there," Juliette clasped her hands in her lap and fixed Justin with a speculative look, "you have my story. Yes, I came from an aristocratic family, but I had a truly shameful past. You, though you do not have an aristocratic family—for how could you, being from a country that does not believe in such things—have a most admirable past and, judging from what I have seen of you, probably a splendid future. So what do you say?"

Justin grinned. "I say you are a sorceress . . . but a good one," he hastened to add, "I do not know how you divined all this when I was barely aware of it myself until very recently, but I do appreciate your understanding and your encouragement. Still, it is very difficult; we are from two different worlds, two different countries, where each of us is tied by family obligations." He sighed, running a hand through thick auburn curls.

'You are entirely correct. There are difficulties. On the other hand, I don't know of two more determined people than you and my sister-in-law. And," she continued as she saw the doubts setting in, "I know that, no matter the obstacles, Georgie will be very unhappy if you return to America without at least speaking to her. It is not simply that she is unlikely to find someone to make her as happy as you would, it is likely that she will be most unhappy without you. Do I make myself clear?"

He nodded slowly. "Perfectly."

"Good! Now go and admire Auguste's equestrian accomplishments, and I leave the rest to you."

Justin rose, bowed, then, taking her hand, raised it to his lips. "Thank you," he whispered, and then he was gone.

CHAPTER 20

JUSTIN FOUND AUGUSTE AND NED IN THE STABLE YARD where Ned was helping the boy up onto Mameluke.

"Mr. Appleton, Mr. Appleton, you came! Mama said you might, but not to count on it because you are a very busy man. But here you are! Come watch me put Mameluke through his paces. He is coming along awfully well, I think."

Ned favored Justin with a broad wink. "Yes sir, we're all doing awfully well. If you could just follow us to the paddock, sir, you can see for yourself. Come on then, lad." The groom headed out of the stable toward the paddock.

It struck Justin how gratified he was by a small boy's excitement simply over his presence. Perhaps someday he would have a son of his own like Auguste. The thought brought Justin up short. He'd never thought of himself in terms of a family, only in terms of his work, but Lady Adrian's revelations had opened up a whole new vista for him, a vista that was increasingly seductive. But now it was time to focus his attention on a boy and his horse, and indeed, it was touching to witness the bond between the two—a tribute to Auguste's aunt as well as Auguste.

After observing a slow canter and a trot around strategically placed objects, Justin could legitimately say, "I am most impressed with you and Mameluke, Auguste. You seem to possess an excellent understanding of good horsemanship."

Auguste beamed, then dismounted into Ned's waiting arms. "Aunt Georgie says I am not to tax him, so I must lead him to his stall now, brush him and feed him and water him so he knows he has done a good job. Come along, Mameluke." He began to lead the horse toward the stables, then, remembering Justin, he turned to him, "and thank you for coming. Thank you too for showing us your manor yesterday. It was most in . . . most in . . . most instructive."

Justin barely stifled the grin that threatened to break out . . . so the ladies had considered the tour of Clinton House *instructive*, had they? Now there was nothing to do but reclaim Brutus before returning home after his own most instructive visit to Ashbourne.

Having been forewarned by his hostess that Georgie was with Mr. Tripp and figuring that Lady Adrian had picked this day on purpose to insure that her sister-in-law would not be around to interrupt their conversation, Justin knew not to expect seeing Georgie, but he couldn't help hoping against hope to catch a glimpse of her, at the very least. Luck was with him, however. As he led Brutus out of the stables, he observed Georgie in the yard at the other end where the Ashbourne racing stock were kept, immersed in deep conversation with Mr. Tripp as he climbed into his gig. Then, with a quick wave as the veterinarian headed out, she turned back toward the stables.

Justin hurried toward her before she could enter the stables. "Lady Georgiana!"

She paused, but he could see her mind was elsewhere. It was a long minute before her abstracted frown turned into recognition. "Mr. Appleton! What are you doing here?"

It was not a very promising beginning. Justin had the sinking feeling that he was intruding as she worked through some issue she and her colleague had been discussing—a lowering thought. Then she smiled. "I *do* beg your pardon. That was rather rag-mannered of me. Of course we are glad to see you here at Ashbourne any time."

"Actually, I came at Lady Adrian's invitation." The flush that had risen to her cheeks when she realized how rude she'd sounded made him feel better. "Apparently Auguste was eager to demonstrate his riding skills since I'd only had the briefest of glimpses of them when I encountered you all the other day on your ride."

"You came to see Auguste ride Mameluke? That was most kind of you."

Justin had her full attention now. "Yes. He is certainly doing very well, though that is hardly surprising, given his aunt's devotion to him and to Mameluke." Justin had never realized just how wonderful it could be to make another person happy, and there was no doubt that Georgie was happy. The glow on her face and the light in her eyes as she took in his words said it all. Her expression, like her conversation, was open, honest, and direct. Lord how he loved her!

What? Where had that sprung from? But Justin knew it was true. Lady Adrian's perceptiveness and her revelations had forced him to recognize it. Now what was he going to do? But at that moment, Georgie was scrutinizing him, curiosity stamped on every feature. There were no flies on her, not his Georgie. She knew something was up. "Ah, I see you were with Mr. Tripp today." It sounded oddly rushed and awkward for the supposedly casual observation he meant to make.

One corner of her mouth lifted as Georgie reveled in his confusion—or whatever it was that made him look and sound ill-at-ease. Justin Appleton was always so big, bold, and self-assured in a way that filled her with envy that Georgie took great pleasure in seeing him thrown off balance. Part of his confidence, she knew, was that he was simply a clever, competent man to whom these things and the respect they commanded came naturally, while she as a woman, especially a *great gawky* one, could not command that respect; if she even hinted so much at being clever, much less competent, she was regarded with dismay rather than admiration.

Then she took pity on him. "Yes, Mr. Tripp and I were dealing with a number of issues: an eye inflamed by a hayseed which we removed and then treated with fomentations, a cut on the shoulder from a protruding nail in a fence which we had to clean and then stitch up—most interesting—and a sprain in a young horse who had been training."

"And you enjoyed every minute, I see." Her enthusiasm was as palpable as it was rewarding to Justin who liked to think he had, had some hand it in.

Georgie grinned. "I did, though no well brought-up young woman should admit to such a thing; not that I ever aspired to be a well brought-up young woman."

He laughed. "No, you apparently do not, rare, fearless individual that you are."

She sobered; blue eyes wide with surprise. "You actually mean that, don't you?"

He reached for her hands, gathering them into his as he looked down at her. "Yes. I do, and so does Mr. Tripp."

"I . . . I never thanked you for that, you know," her voice grew husky, "not only for believing that it is worth wanting something desperately, but for divining what it was that I wanted desperately, even before I did, and then making that dream happen." She withdrew her hands to dash away a tear that would seep out of the corner of her eye. "And now I have turned into a complete watering pot, blast you! I am *never* a watering pot, especially not because of some man!"

Justin retrieved her hand and pulled her toward him. "Georgie . . . er Lady Georgiana, I hope you can see by now that I would do anything to help you achieve your dream, I would do anything for you, for you are the dearest . . ." He could not go on. What else was there to say or do except wrap his arms around her and press his lips to hers, pouring his entire soul into his kiss.

Georgie melted against him, her lips opening under his as he claimed her for his own . . . as he felt her claiming him right back, his bold and determined Georgie; it was not enough. When had physical connection been enough, Justin asked himself, even though he knew the answer—when there was such a thing as love, something his skeptical, questioning mind had doubted existed until now. He gripped her shoulders, setting her back a little so he could search her face, looking for answers in those compellingly straightforward eyes. "I love you, Georgie, with all my heart. I love you, and with all my being I honor you. And I can think of nothing more wonderful than to spend the rest of my life with you."

The compellingly straightforward eyes were now alight with joy, the lips parting in a tender, tremulous smile just for him, Justin Appleton, brash American. "You complete me. You are my soulmate." His face twisted. "But I will not distract you from your goal. You must stay here, study under Mr. Tripp, become all you can be, and I," his voice was raw, "I must return to America to fulfill the promise I made to my father. I do not know what to do." Justin Appleton had never uttered those words in his life, never even entertained the thought that he might find himself at a loss for a solution to a problem, any problem.

"Nor do I," Georgie's lips quirked in rueful smile—another determined soul as much at a loss as he was, "but I expect that between the two of us, we will come up with a solution. Lead on!"

The two of us! We! Solution! That's what they were, problem-solvers, both of them, willing to tackle difficult questions on their own; now they could do it together. How he adored this woman!

Justin grinned back. "Whatever you say, my love. I rely on you to come up with our solution." Giving her a final kiss, he threw himself into the saddle and headed toward the drive, his heart filled with joy and his mind alight with the possibilities for the future.

CHAPTER 21

GEORGIE WAS MORE THAN READY TO LEAD ON, though she had no idea how to solve the impossible complex situation Justin had just laid before them, but she did know it would involve a great deal of thought and exploration—and *exploration*—which, after that heady embrace, was something she eagerly looked forward to, hours of exploration, one heart-stopping kiss at a time. Oh that broad chest—the one she had dreamed of flinging herself against since the very first moment she had come upon the jacketless Justin at his anvil. She had wanted him then, though, at the time, she had not understood what the racing heart and ecstatic breathlessness were about. Now she did, and she wanted more, everything, all of him.

For now, there was something else that demanded her immediate, though now reluctant, attention—the wedding of her dear Verena and even dearer Freddy. Loyal friend and loving sister that she was, Georgie could not ignore the upcoming nuptials simply because she herself had suddenly discovered what love was, that, despite her cynical doubts, love did, in fact, exist.

Verena and Freddy's wedding at Carstairs Hall in Bedfordshire had been finally set for the coming week. Given the bride's retiring nature and the family's straightened circumstances, it was to be a small affair, which meant that the guests who were invited—only the families on both sides—were being relied on for not only their presence, but their enthusiastic support, or that was how Georgie saw it at least. As the one responsible for the successful conclusion of the match in the first place, Georgie felt it incumbent upon her to do her utmost to make it a very special day for everyone. This did not mean, as it would have for anyone else, fretting about selecting the most suitable costume for the occasion, but it meant making sure that Auguste, thought naturally not invited to the ceremony, would be allowed to accompany his parents, thereby insuring that they would look forward wholeheartedly to the event with none of the reservations they might feel leaving him in the expert care of nurse and the devoted staff at Ashbourne, or of strangers at Carstairs Hall. It also meant encouraging her brother John to offer his services as officiant, should they be needed, and answering any and all of Verena's questions as to the family's preferences in accommodation and dining.

Georgie explained this all to Justin in some detail when she and Ned encountered him on a quick ride meant to clear the cobwebs from her brain. Georgie had just given Nero his head and was galloping across the fields when she heard the pounding of hooves behind her, and suddenly Brutus and Nero were neck and neck.

Tossing her head, she leaned low over Nero's shoulders, urging him forward. There was a shout of laughter behind her as Justin caught up with her and slowly inched ahead. It was no use. Brutus was larger and faster than Nero, and she was going to shame her best equine friend by losing an unequal contest, so she gently slowed the pace.

"You ride as though all the hounds of hell are after you. Poor Ned must be miles behind."

Georgie laughed and shook her head, blond curls escaping from under her modish riding hat. "I was just clearing my head of wedding details."

"Wedding details?" Even though he would have loved to think she was referring to him and her, Justin was not that naïve, no matter how madly he wanted it to be true.

"My brother Freddy and my closest friend, Verena."

"Ah." Comprehension dawned. "The union you so cleverly brought about."

She had the grace to blush. Yes she *did* manage people, but it was only in the nicest way and in their best interests. "They make a perfect couple. Verena is sensible and kind, unlike Freddy's previous fiancée who was a . . ." she clapped a gloved hand over her mouth, "well, anyway, Verena loves gardening and has designed the grounds at Carstairs Hall beautifully, and Freddy has artistic talents of his own, having spent an age improving Wrothingham Abbey, but they remain unappreciated by the rest of us who are not artistically inclined. Besides, Verena's father, the Earl of Carstairs, is one of Papa's oldest friends. He and Lord Wolverton and Papa were at Eton together and are closer than most brothers, though Lord Carstairs is very quiet and scholarly, spending most of his time in the library at Carstairs Hall while Papa and Lord Wolverton are both devoted to politics and spend much of their time in London. After the wedding, everyone is stopping at Ashbourne on their way to Claverton. Good heavens, I am carrying on like a perfect jaw-me-dead. I am sure you have not the least interest in such things, but well . . . I want them to be happy so I am doing my best to help with what I can."

"On the contrary, I am very interested in all of it. You are such a close family, and you, from what I can see, are the most devoted and loyal of them all." And he loved her for that dedicated, if managing, devotion.

There was a wistful note in Justin's voice that tugged at Georgie's heart. She never really thought about her family—they were just there—but when she saw the shadow of loneliness in his eyes, she realized how fortunate she was that they all rubbed along tolerably well together, and (not that it was necessarily expressed) that they cared what happened to her as she cared what happened to them. When she thought about it Georgie realized that, by and large, they genuinely enjoyed one another's company. "Loyal and devoted, yes," she raised her chin, "obedient? Not particularly."

Justin laughed, remembering John's stories of his sister's tree-climbing exploits, then he sobered. "I will miss you when you are gone. Life is very dull without you, you know, and I . . ."

Whatever tantalizing remark he was about to make was cut short by the arrival of Ned; long-suffering writ large on his face as he urged Bess forward. It would have been tantalizing, Georgie knew from the sly, slightly self-conscious smile playing around his mouth and the way his eyes fixed on her lips and then traveled slowly, suggestively along her jawline to the tender spot just under her ear where he knew just what to do to make her ache with longing.

Justin glanced at Ned. "I think, seeing that Nero has stopped throwing that challenging look at Brutus, that I had best be going so that Ned and Bess have a chance to catch their breaths." With one last, lingering look at those lips which had opened under his hungry gaze, he pressed his knees into Brutus' flank, and they trotted off towards Clinton House, leaving Georgie gasping as though she'd actually been smothered in his powerful embrace instead of fantasizing about it.

She continued to fantasize during the entire tedious journey to Carstairs Hall. Ordinarily it would not have been tedious, what with Auguste bouncing about with excitement and Adrian and Juliette taking turns at telling tall tales until he fell asleep at last, but lately, every place that was not in Justin's arms seemed tedious to Georgie.

No sooner had they finally arrived at Carstairs Hall and been welcomed by joyous family members and soon-to-be family members than Georgie found herself longing to climb right back in the carriage and return to Ashbourne—in truth, return to Clinton House rather than Ashbourne, Clinton House where Justin had put that beautiful library completely at her disposal, omniscient man that he was. How else could he have known that the room was the sort of place she would relish settling in and reading to her heart's content? How else would he have known it was the perfect size, the perfect view through perfect windows looking out over the fields if he couldn't read her mind, as he had done so many times before? He seemed to know what she wanted and needed before she did, like books on equine anatomy, or learning first-hand from Mr. Tripp how to minister to sick and injured horses.

Then, there was the complication whose solution he had dumped in her lap. He wanted to be with her. Well, she wanted to be with him—desperately so—but he wanted her to continue with her studies with Mr. Tripp so that she could become what she had not even dared to dream of becoming before knowing Mr. Justin Appleton. He had made it perfectly clear, with his assumption that she would remain at Ashbourne continuing her studies while he returned to America, that he believed in her and her capabilities and expected her to develop them. He hadn't even begged her to come with him, which was rather unflattering when one got right down to it. If one were in love, wouldn't the prospect of living without the person they loved be unbearably lonely and agonizing?

Yes. It would be. It was. Georgie's heart squeezed painfully, and her throat clogged at the very thought of it. Justin seemed to assume that she could bear it for the sake of fulfilling her dreams, just as he would bear it for the sake of fulfilling his father's. She had seen the sympathy and trust in his eyes and heard the confidence in his voice as he handed the responsibility of solving their future over to her, Georgie Claverton, a young woman whose only experience of life was a privileged one. It made her unbelievably proud to be treated with such respect, such faith in her judgment. It made her feel like . . . well, like an equal. What other man had even treated her as anything but a female, a mindless female, who was not very decorative, but well connected and wealthy enough to have that drawback overlooked?

CHAPTER 22

NOW, HOWEVER, ALL EYES WERE ON Verena and Freddy, and Georgie, who was really very happy for both of them, was forced to focus her attention on the wedding, like the good sister and devoted friend she was. As she watched Freddy greeting his family and Verena's in the drawing room before dinner, she thought she'd never seen him so at ease, so comfortable in who he truly was—not the heir to the Duke of Roxburgh, but Freddy Claverton, connoisseur, appreciator of beauty in all its forms, and a creator of beauty in his own right. It seemed he had encountered a kindred spirit not only in Verena, with her passion for gardening, but in her brother, William, an architect whose taste was completely in tune with his sister's and his prospective brother-in-law's.

In fact, the trio, deep in discussion, soon seemed to drift slightly apart from the familial crowd. "William and Frederick are designing me a conservatory at Wrothingham Abbey," Verena explained when Georgie, in her forthright way, could not help commenting on it.

"Finally, someone is taking you seriously." Georgie grinned. It was so nice to see how Freddy's understanding and respect for Verena's talents had given her friend confidence. It was a little thing, but Verena now moved with quiet assurance among the small gathering with none of the hanging back or self-deprecating expression that used to diminish her features and make her appear more plain than she actually was, as well as just a touch insipid.

Georgie didn't know if others acquainted with Verena would have noticed the transformation, but it made Georgie very happy. Finally now she completely understood how such a thing could come about—not that Georgie had ever been self-deprecating—but Justin's confidence in her had given her a belief in herself that she had never possessed before. Yes, she had always been strong-minded in pursuing the happiness and wellbeing of the humans and horses close to her, but she had never actually felt sure of her own capabilities and worth until a certain handsome American had pointed them out to her and then made sure she nurtured them.

Freddy's laugh broke into these reflections, and Georgie glanced up in surprise as she realized that she had never actually her older brother laugh before. He was grinning at Verena's brother who, judging from the teasing smirk on his face, must have provoked it.

"You look taken aback—not a common thing for my redoubtable sister who never lets anyone get the jump on her." John appeared at her side. "What are you thinking?"

"Just that I have never heard Freddy laugh, I mean really, truly laugh."

John sobered. "You do have a point there. William and Verena have brought out the joy in him." He looked over at the trio, seeing far more than his sister who was much less familiar with the vast complexity of human nature than her ministering brother did. *What an extraordinary woman!* John thought as he read the fond smile with which Verena watched her brother and fiancée in their lively conversation, and he resolved to tell her so at the first possible moment.

The opportunity arose when the men joined the women after dinner and Verena led her elder brother over to where John and Georgie were again comparing notes. "I know that you and Henry have been introduced already," she greeted Georgie, "but you are very formidable, and Henry is of such a retiring nature that he will not put himself forward," she darted a teasing glance at the hapless Henry, "something I, myself, understand completely, as you well know. Besides being bookish, which will interest your brother here far more than it does you, he is a consummate horseman who has one or two burning questions about the behavior of his latest mount, Pegasus that he should pose to you."

Henry favored Georgie with a shy smile. "The issue at hand is that he does not in the least live up to his name, but I purchased him anyway because he is a superb creature physically and should out-perform any horse in the field, but something holds him back, which, I suspect, can be diagnosed by someone cleverer than I in no time."

"There!" Verena chuckled, turning to John, "that should keep the two of them occupied for a good long time."

"Are you taking a leaf out of my sister's book?" John raised a quizzical brow.

"Good heavens! I am not nearly so managing as Georgie. It is just that Henry so often gets quite overlooked, and a little of Georgie's bracing attitude would do him a world of good."

"As you have done for my brother. I have never seen him look so happy; I think." His eyes sought out Freddy and William, heads together, bent over what appeared to be a drawing.

"Oh, that would be the conservatory they are designing for me. It was William's idea and Wrothingham so very kindly and enthusiastically entered into the scheme. We are looking forward to having William make his home with us at Wrothingham Abbey when he is not in London or wherever his work takes him."

"An excellent idea." John fixed her with a penetrating gaze, and what he saw in her face answered all his questions. Taking her hand in his, he raised it to his lips. "And you are the most perceptive, intelligent, and generous of women. It is an honor to know you, and an even greater one to call you my future sister-in-law. I do hope this union makes you as happy as it makes my brother."

"It does. I have a true friend of the heart and companion in the love of design in your brother, and he has pledged his life to making me happy. What woman could ask for anything more?"

True romantic love, John thought, but he was not sure that even he believed in such a thing, despite what he'd seen in Adrian and Juliette when they looked at one another, and the same electric connection between Juliette's friends Grace and Helen and their husbands. The straightforward way, though, in which Verena met his gaze reassured him that she asked for nothing more than she had and treasured it with all her heart.

The honest, unflinching gaze warmed into a smile that John could have sworn hinted at the conspiratorial as Verena added, "And it does my heart good to see how much he and William enjoy one another's company as they enter into this joint project."

Ah yes, John thought, *a remarkably intelligent and sensitive woman indeed!* How fortunate they were to have her in the family. He whispered as much to Georgie the next day as Verena entered the family chapel on her father's arm.

"I am not stupid, you know," she muttered *sotto voce,* "I knew what I was doing."

For others, perhaps, but for yourself? John wondered. The previous evening he had observed his sister's conversation with Henry, but though it had been friendly enough, Georgie had not displayed the vivacity with him that she did with Justin Appleton, and it was immediately clear to John that Viscount Sanford was destined to remain the eldest brother of his sister's good friend, and nothing more, while Justin Appleton, John sensed, was something altogether different, a potent, if unknown force in his sister's life.

For confirmation of his suspicions, he sought out his sister-in-law who, besides having recently lived in closer proximity to Georgie, was almost as skilled an observer and interpreter of human nature as he was.

John managed to pull Juliette aside right after the wedding breakfast as the guests were offering their congratulations to the bride and groom and assorted family members. "Tell me if I am correct in thinking there is a movement afoot, at least on the part of my newest sister-in-law, to throw Georgie and Viscount Sanford together as much as possible."

"Oh undoubtedly."

"And tell me if I am also correct in thinking he does not stand a chance when compared to a certain American gentleman of our acquaintance."

Juliette's eyebrows rose. "You *are* a deep one, are you not?"

It was a subtle evasion of his question, but the faintest pink tinging Juliette's cheeks made John suspect that there was even more to be learned from this line of questioning. "Hmmm, I detect something deeper here than mere conjecture, out with it, dear sister-in-law."

"In spite of being a man of the cloth, you are never one to let a woman enjoy her secrets," Juliette pouted.

"And?"

"Very well! And I have eyes in my head, I see what Mr. Justin Appleton has done for Georgie, what he has given her. I can see they are meant for one another—soulmates, one might say."

If anyone could appreciate the discovery of a soulmate, it was Juliette, John thought as he recalled—almost enviously—a hundred special looks and smiles exchanged between his brother and his wife. "Of course, being you, you didn't stop with a simple observation," he shook his head, smiling. "I know you; you are almost as energetic in the promotion of the happiness of those you care about as Georgie."

The pink darkened in Juliette's cheeks, spreading into a deep flush over her entire face. "Well, I *did* intimate to Mr. Appleton that the Clavertons are not so high in the instep and exclusive as he might think where men lacking aristocratic credentials, but possessing tremendous character and intelligence were concerned."

John choked back a laugh. "Of course, you did."

"I certainly did not want him to return to America without telling Georgie how much he cared for her—the only man in whom she has evinced the slightest interest. It would be devastating to her." Juliette was indignant now.

"And you were absolutely in the right of it. But tell me now, what you make of the plot to throw Georgie and Viscount Sanford together?"

"Absurd," she scoffed. "Just look at him—dullish hair, not even an ounce of character, or enthusiasm in his face, no physical presence whatsoever. Perfectly nice, of course, and not dimwitted or puffed up with his own consequence as so many are who have irritated Georgie beyond bearing, but not up to her weight at all. She would be bored within a week, and there's nothing he can give her that she does not already possess, whereas Mr. Appleton challenges her; he inspires her to follow her dreams, to better herself, and, he is, er, a fine figure of a man." She wagged her finger at John, "And don't think she hasn't noticed. I have seen how she looks at him."

John rubbed his jaw thoughtfully. "So have I." And then his mother was at his side asking him if he thought he would join them in their carriage as part of the little group planning to stop at Ashbourne Hall on the way to Claverton.

"Do you know, I think I shall."

The duchess patted his shoulder and then was off to re-join her husband as they circled among the group of well-wishers while Juliette favored him with a conspiratorial smile. "Your company could be most useful to me, should I need it."

"I am deeply honored, Lady Adrian, and always at your service," the twinkle in his eyes belied his formal bow."

CHAPTER 23

JULIETTE FOUND IT TELLING THAT HER SISTER-IN-LAW was far more vivacious and engaged on the return trip to Ashbourne than she had been on the departing. Upon their arrival home, she bounced out of the carriage and up the steps as though she had not just spent endless hours trying to mollify a cranky five-year-old who was tired

If the day hadn't been so advanced and the ploy so obvious, Georgie would have saddled up Nero and headed off in the hopes of encountering the master of Clinton House, but she was forced to contain her eagerness but that night, she lay awake devising schemes to run into Justin without actually calling on him, which would have been a move too bold even for Georgie.

Fortunately for her peace of mind, the next morning as she was sitting in the library with Juliette going over plans for the amusement of their soon-to-be guests, Wilson appeared to announce, "Mr. Appleton, my lady."

"Do send him in, please." Juliette stifled a smile at the transformation of Georgie from a dutiful sister-in-law, tepidly interested in the plans under discussion, to bright-eyed young woman eager to welcome their guest.

"Forgive me for intruding on you so soon after your return," *(But I could stay away no longer)* Justin apologized completely unapologetically, his eyes fixing on Georgie as if she had been gone for a twelvemonth instead of a matter of days, "but I bring news which might be of interest to Lady Georgiana."

From the look on Georgie's face, he, and he alone, was of interest to her as she sat there grinning until Juliette was forced to answer for her. "Pray, do sit down and tell us your news."

It was a moment before her words sank in. At last, Justin, equally distracted, responded. "Oh, er, yes, my ship has returned from New York and Captain Kincade Webb reports that Mr. Talbot has been safely deposited on American soil and is at present in New York City, under the watchful eye of several stout fellows who work at our docks, so I doubt he will be able to cause too much trouble, as they know every trick in the book and have spread word far and wide that he is a man to watch oneself with."

"That is excellent news!" Georgie beamed. "I must tell Ned who also took quite a dislike to the man. Thank you for coming to tell us."

"I am happy to be the bearer of good news and let us hope that it is the last we hear of Nathan Talbot. But I imagine you also have happy news to relate. I trust the wedding went well."

"Oh yes. In fact, we," Georgie turned to Juliette with a significant look, "were just discussing the arrival of the wedding party here on their way to Claverton."

Juliette took the hint. "We have been thinking of having an *al fresco* Venetian breakfast on the terrace—a most informal affair, you understand—and we would be delighted if you could join us. My brother-in-law, John, will be here, as well as Wrothingham and his new bride, and of course my parents-in-law, so you will get to meet the entire family. It should not be too overwhelming as you have already met its most intimidating member," she nodded at Georgie, daring her to contradict her but Georgie only laughed. "Oh no, Mama is far more imposing than I."

"But you are young yet, give yourself time," Justin interjected with a wicked smile and Juliette laughed, glad to see that he was not above teasing her sister-in-law. It spoke of a fondness and intimacy between the two that did her heart good.

"Oh goodness, I promised Auguste that I would watch him put Mameluke through his paces. Do join us, Mr. Appleton, we shan't be long." Juliette rose and headed toward the door, closing it behind her.

There! That should give them some precious time alone together. She then took her time making her way down the hall and up the stairs to the nursery.

Georgie and Justin stood for a moment reveling in being together again; then Justin closed the gap between them, pulling her into his arms. "I am only an uncouth American who cannot help speaking his mind brazenly, and I can tell you that I missed you, but I would rather prove it."

He crushed her to him with a hunger that left Georgie in no doubt that he had missed her sorely, and she reveled in it. When had she ever felt so loved, so desired . . . so precious to another person? Heretofore, she had only felt important to the horses she loved and cared for, but this? This was heaven! To look up into his eyes and see the love and, yes, even adoration, to press herself against him and feel how much he wanted her made her heart—and other less respectable parts of her body—ache with love and desire. She was overwhelmed with the urge to tear off her clothes so she could feel his hands sliding from her waist to her breasts, his palms cupping them, caressing her bare skin instead of several layers of muslin. To think that before she'd met Justin Appleton, she'd never entertained such thoughts at all, never even dreamed of kissing a man as so many of her schoolmates had done to an utterly boring degree.

She gave herself up to the heat of his lips on hers that demanded so many answers and pulled his head down to drink in the taste and smell of him. Yes, she had missed him too. She hadn't known how much until she again drank in his overwhelming physical presence, a physical presence that had mesmerized her and drawn her to him irresistibly since the moment she had laid eyes on him.

At last, he lifted his head. "Clinton House is empty and cold, listless and dull without the hope of seeing you." Justin marveled at himself. Was this the man who scorned pretty speeches or sharing any part of himself with a woman? But what a woman! Georgie deserved to know just how incredible she was, how precious she was to him, and how she filled his life.

The sound of pounding feet and an eager voice asking, "You said Mr. Appleton came to see me and Mameluke?" broke them apart, but not before Justin could say, "I look forward to meeting and talking with the rest of your family . . . especially your father."

There was no mistaking the significance of the look he gave her, and Georgie's heart pounded. He could speak to her father, but that didn't address the fact that he had business in America, and the only way for her to pursue the dream he had given her was for her to remain here in England studying with Mr. Tripp. In such a short space of time she had been given two unexpectedly and unimaginably wonderful visions for her future . . . and they were tearing her apart. She desperately wanted them both. *Think, Georgie, think! He is relying on you to come up with a solution. Now do it!*

CHAPTER 24

GEORGIE SPENT A RESTLESS NIGHT, TORTURED not so much by the solution she was tasked with coming up with, but with the memories of Justin's arms, his broad chest, his lips searching and arousing in a desperate quest for more, more, more!

The next day, with its prospect of visitors, brought welcome distraction as Georgie and Juliette made sure that rooms were aired, beds and pillow fluffed, and everything laid out for the comfort of their guests who arrived hungry and tired in time for dinner which soon revived spirits, reminiscences of the wedding, and discussions of projects and plans for the future.

Justin had spent the day riding through the fields, and as the afternoon faded had caught sight of the procession on the road from the village just as it arrived at the gates of Ashbourne. The next day he witnessed a party on horseback exploring Ashbourne's own fields and pastures. He easily recognized John and Adrian, their blond heads gleaming in the sun, and there was no mistaking his own bold Amazon on Nero, but who was the nondescript fellow at her side whose mount's uninspiring gait did not live up to the promise of its handsome appearance? Was this the third brother, Freddy, as Georgie called him? He did not have the look of a Claverton—far too unprepossessing—even though Georgie had told him that Freddy's talents and tastes tended toward the artistic rather than the sporting.

The pair did seem to be on excellent terms, however, so it must be a relative of some sort.

Knowing he would be introduced to everyone the next day at the Venetian breakfast, Justin put it out of his mind and concentrated on answering a letter from Mr. Telford inviting him to the next meeting of the newly founded Institute of Civil Engineers, of which he was president. It was indeed a flattering invitation, one which, at any other time, would have thrilled him beyond measure, but with Georgie newly returned it was a great deal less appealing than it would have been to the Justin Appleton who had never met Lady Georgiana Claverton. What had become of that engineering-obsessed man? Oddly enough, even though that man had disappeared, Justin did not miss him.

As Justin had expected the question as to the identity of Georgie's fellow rider was answered the next day at the Venetian breakfast. Juliette had just introduced him to the Duke and Duchess of Roxburgh as they were all gathered on the terrace while the servants put the finishing touches on the food-laden tables when Georgie and the same fellow—deep in conversation—emerged from a path leading from the stables.

Justin's attention was so immediately drawn to them that he almost missed replying to the Duchess' question about what he had learned on his visit to Telford's canal. As it was, it was a most lackluster reply for a man who had journeyed to England in search of inspiration about canal construction. *Yes, he'd learned a great deal. Yes, he was impressed by the steam engine and a new measuring tool that had been shown him.* Still, it was flattering that the Duchess knew that much about him, and even more flattering that she must have heard it from her daughter.

He was saved further embarrassingly dull responses by the appearance of Georgie's brother and his new bride. The Marquess of Wrothingham had the same fair hair and blue eyes as his brothers and sister, but where their gazes were penetrating, his was open and guileless, his almost chubby features seeming to express a shyness unknown to his siblings. The new marchioness, on the other hand, had all the obvious energy and determined character apparently lacking in her spouse. A complimentary couple, Justin decided. Georgie had known what she was about in matching them up. He could certainly see how a woman of such strong personality as the new Lady Wrothingham and Georgie had become fast friends at school.

Verena saw Justin's eyes stray back to Georgie and her companion. "My brother Henry, Viscount Sanford," she remarked, smiling fondly at the pair. Then she lowered her voice to a confidential whisper. "We are hoping for another family announcement soon. So lovely to look forward to having Georgie even more closely allied to the Carstairs family. He will be perfect for her. He is scholarly and kind and not at all full of himself as so many of these men are, and she will be good for him too. She will make a wonderful countess, just as her mother is an excellent duchess."

Justin was unprepared for the sharp bolt of pain that shot through his heart. He was not an emotional man, had always been a man of science and rational thought, but this! It left him groping for his next breath. Georgie hadn't even told him about this man. How could she not have mentioned him even in passing? Yet here they were on such friendly terms as though they'd known one another forever . . . and perhaps they had.

But at that moment, Juliette came over to urge them all to the feast and Justin was left to join them as though his entire world had not just been blown apart. Juliette, her intuition sharpened after years at Mrs. Gerrard's reading men's unspoken wants and desires, saw the devastation in Justin's eyes as they followed her sister-in-law, laid her hand on his arm. "She is just being kind to him, bookish recluse that he is, and they have a mutual topic of interest in his underperforming horse—so like Mameluke." Then she was off to gather up the rest of the guests.

Justin blessed her for her sensitivity and her sympathy, and he trusted implicitly her reading of the situation, but it gave him pause. He spent the rest of the evening responding in a most perfunctory manner to the conversations that swirled around him, and later that night tossing and turning in an agony of soul-searching and self-examination, going over and over again in his mind every minute he had spent with Georgie, from her first open-mouthed, wide-eyed encounter with him in his smithy to the breathless, devouring kissed they had exchanged when he had called on her to give her the news about Talbot.

He remembered the way John and Adrian had teased her at that first dinner at Ashbourne, the pride with which Adrian had introduced John to him, the devotion she had showed to both her school friend and her eldest brother by bringing them together to enjoy their shared interests and one another. And now he wanted to take her away from all that, not only from her country, but her beloved family. How could he do that, especially when he had no warm and loving family to offer in return? In fact, he had spent so much of his life immersed in his scientific and engineering passions that he had few social circles, other than scientific ones, into which to introduce her. To be sure, he had many acquaintances, some he even called friends, but they were men in the shipping and canal-building businesses, and they, like him, had all been too committed to their projects to introduce him to their own wives and families.

Now, here came a man, an aristocrat in his own right, (not that Justin believed that titles conferred anything special to their bearers, but they did mean the owner was part of Georgie's world, the only world she had ever known) and the brother of her closest friend who wanted to make her his wife. How could Justin gratify his own selfish desire for love and companionship by standing in the way of such future happiness for Lady Georgiana Claverton? No, he could not! He loved her too much to do that. Tomorrow he would prove it. Tomorrow, he would show her that he was strong enough to face life without her in order that she could spend the rest of hers surrounded by family and loved ones.

Fortunately, Justin had an excuse to appear at Ashbourne the next day. John had invited him for a game of chess. "Not that you are my most formidable or challenging opponent," he chuckled, "but it has been some time since I have had any opportunity or leisure to play at all."

"Any port in a storm, eh?" Justin grinned, flattered that Georgie's brother considered him enough of a friend to tease him with the brutal truth about his chess-playing abilities.

But as they sat down to play, John knew it was not only not going to be a challenging game, but it was also going to be a decidedly insipid one. His opponent's face was unwontedly somber, even for a serious game, and his plays were erratic at best—mindless at worst. Something of deep importance was clearly occupying the thoughts of the man facing him across the chessboard, and he'd never seen Justin Appleton, man of science and business and complicated affairs not fully in control and alive to the moment. Even his thanks for the game and his farewell were haphazard as he brushed aside all offers to call for his mount and headed towards the stables himself.

The stables! That was it. John shook his head at his own stupidity. Justin was hoping to find Georgie there. Had they had a falling out? John hadn't noticed one, but then, people had been milling about at the Venetian breakfast and he had been preoccupied with talking with all of them. He would have to consult with Juliette to see if she could offer any insight.

CHAPTER 25

JUSTIN WAS IN LUCK. GEORGIE WAS IN NERO'S STALL brushing him while the guests were off admiring Adrian's blood stock. She was savoring the respite from the constant company and conversation surrounding her and demanding her attention since the wedding party had arrived.

The sound of approaching footsteps broke her concentration, informing her that her moment of peace and quiet was about to be interrupted. Bother! She swiped an unruly curl from her face in annoyance. Then she caught sight of a tall shadow on the opposite wall. Only one man was tall enough to make such a shadow, Justin! She dropped her brush and held out her hands.

Justin gripped them in both of his, warm, strong and steady, as always, but his face was grave . . . and pale. He looked more like some marble statue than her ruggedly handsome American who made her blood heat every time she saw him. "Is something amiss?"

He was silent for a moment, devouring her with his amber gaze. "Amiss? Ah, er no . . . but" he drew a quick breath, released her hands, and then plunged ahead, frowning as though trying to recall the exact words he had prepared some time before he appeared. "I happened to fall into conversation with Lady Wrothingham at the Venetian breakfast yesterday, and . . ."

"Did you like her? Did you get a chance to see how sensible and intelligent she is? I do think she and Freddy will do extremely well together, and . . ." Georgie faltered, realizing she'd interrupted him in the midst of something he had been about to say, something that seemed to be so important it made her nervous.

"Yes, I could see she is a woman of great good sense which is why I took her words so seriously."

"Words? What words?"

"That she hoped, no, that she expected to be welcoming you into the family soon."

Her utterly blank expression lightened the dark cloud that had filled Justin's soul the moment those words had been uttered. So she wasn't in love with Sanford, for surely a woman in love, or even one with a special connection to the brother of her dear friend, would have looked more conscious than Georgie did. Indeed, she appeared genuinely bewildered.

"She seems to expect to hear an announcement of your engagement to her brother in the near future."

"Whaaaaat? Sanford? How on earth could she think such a thing? I barely know him!" She did look, not only taken aback, but affronted, Justin rejoiced to see, but then he remembered the purpose of his mission which was about her and her future and not him, Justin Appleton, and whether she cared about him—which he was just selfish enough to hope she did—but he also knew it was entirely possible that when away from her family, isolated in a strange land, she might just stop caring for him. "You *did* say she was sensible and intelligent, and I have heard you speak of her as someone who knows you well."

"Not that well if she thinks I'll marry her brother. And what business is it of hers?"

Justin refrained from pointing out that it was because of Georgie's making her friend's happiness *her* business that the wedding party was visiting Ashbourne. "The business of someone who cares for your happiness, who treasures your friendship and longs for greater connection, who must know that her brother, whom she calls *scholarly* and *kind* and not like all those self-important men who irritate you so, is a good match for you."

Georgie stared at him in disbelief which, again, gladdened his heart, but then her eyes darkened, and her lips thinned into an uncompromising line. "And you believe this?" It came out as a rough gasp, ragged around the edges with an emotion he could not interpret. "You thought *I* would marry to make my friend happy, to be allied with . . . I cannot believe it of you! You, who I thought knew me better than anyone, you who I thought understood my hopes, my dreams . . ." She gasped for breath, and now Justin knew the emotion—she was blazingly angry.

"But Lady . . . Georgie," he reached for her shoulder only to have it angrily twitched away, "I *do* understand all that—your hopes and dreams—which you can still have, only you can remain here, studying with Mr. Tripp, surrounded by your family . . ." Her eyes grew darker and darker, her jaw set tighter and tighter. "I care for you, so naturally I only want what is best for you, and . . ."

"And I thought I *loved* you! I thought I had found someone who trusted me to know myself, to know my own mind, but no," she spat, "you are just like the rest of them. *Oh Georgie is so impulsive, she can't be trusted to know what's good for her. She needs a man to look after her.* Well, I will tell you, the only one Georgie Claverton needs to look after her is Georgie Claverton! And," she reached a shaking hand to stroke Nero's nose, "Nero, the only one who has ever loved me, ever *truly* loved me!"

He opened his mouth to swear his own love for her, but before he could utter the words, she turned on her heel and strode out of the stall and towards the far pasture, away from everyone and everything, away from him.

Justin shook his head, reeling from her anger and the look of betrayal in her eyes. He had meant to show her that her happiness meant more to him than anything else, that he would sacrifice his own happiness for hers. Instead he had come across as just another patronizing male, no better than all the other men she railed at in her life, and, worse yet, he had not only hurt her, he had let her down, the one person he had sworn to support in her dreams and aspirations. His eyes stung with the misery of it all as he retrieved Brutus, saddled him up, and headed somberly back towards Clinton House where he could sink into a chair surrounded by the drawings and notes that offered some proof, at least that he was good at something besides bringing fury and misery to the one person in the world he cherished above everything.

But when he arrived at Clinton House, a recently returned Jim Harrington was waiting for him, a travel-stained letter in his hands. "Kincade Webb gave this to me to give to you when I was in London picking up the items you requested, he bring on his return from America."

"Thank you." Justin took it and headed to the library without another word and a brusqueness that was so unlike him that his childhood friend glanced at him sharply before deciding he was best left alone to whatever dark thoughts were obviously troubling him.

Justin sank into his usual chair, staring blankly into the empty grate in the fireplace before halfheartedly glancing at the missive. Whatever was in it could wait until tomorrow. Then he caught sight of the handwriting. No wonder Jim had been waiting to hand it to him. The writing on the envelope was as familiar to him as his own. It was his mother's . . . his dead mother's! Over the years Jim had executed enough commissions for Mrs. Appleton that he too recognized the author of the letter.

Slowly, carefully, Justin undid the seal. Something heavy and hard fell into his lap. He reached for it, holding it up to the light streaming in through the window. It was a ring, a ring with a crest on it.

He smoothed the letter on his lap and began to read. *My dear Justin, my Dearest Son, If you are reading this, I have been gone a year, and only now do I have the courage to tell you the true story behind your birth and my journey to America.*

CHAPTER 26

BREATHING HARD AFTER HER FLIGHT ACROSS THE PASTURE, Georgie stared into the distance, focusing on the wood beyond as she tried to calm herself while struggling to swallow tears of rage or overwhelming grief—she didn't know which. Was she furious at discovering that someone she had thought so gloriously unique and strong in his own beliefs was no different from everyone else—he just came from a country where they were less obvious about following tradition and social systems? Or was she in despair at the loss of the one person she had thought truly loved and respected her?

How had Justin Appleton gone from counting on her to find the solution for the rest of their lives and their happiness to deciding what he thought was best for her life and her happiness? What was she to do now? Georgie had never felt so lost in her life.

Then she heard the pounding of many hooves and watched in awe as Adrian's wounded warriors from Waterloo formed themselves into a formidable dark equine line and charged an invisible enemy, as they often did. These wonderful animals had not given up, neither would she! She would throw every bit of herself into caring for them and for every other sick or injured horse whose pain she could ease with the knowledge and skills she was learning from Mr. Tripp.

Mr. Tripp. A sob rose in her throat at the thought of him. It was Justin who had given her Mr. Tripp. Well now she was going to prove that he had been right to do so; she was going to make her devotion to horses her entire life and her entire happiness—not marriage to some *eligible suitor*, no matter who that suitor was or who thought that suitor was eligible.

With a sigh, but her chin raised, Georgie turned back toward the Hall, the sinking sun telling her the others would be returning and expecting her join them. But as she headed back through the gardens nearest the stables, she heard her name being called. It was Sanford, back from the pasture where they'd been learning all about Adrian's racing stock.

"Lady Georgiana, I am so glad I caught you," Henry favored her with a shy smile, "we have been seeing all that your brother has done with his horses and all he has managed to accomplish in creating such an admirable establishment in such a short while. And," he cocked his head, "I hear you are studying to be of assistance to your brother in his endeavor."

Not quite that, Georgie thought, *I am going to be my own endeavor,* but she gave him credit for trying to understand and she smiled and nodded in reply.

"As to that," Henry drew a deep breath, "I know you have your interests and all, as I have mine," he added with a nervous laugh, "but I was wondering . . ." his voice trailed off, "I mean, my sister speaks so highly of you, and you and she are such friends that I thought you and I might deal well together too."

"You mean friends?" Georgie knew she was being deliberately obtuse, but she wished he'd just say what he meant, that he'd be honest and forthright like . . ." she shoved the thought of *him* from her mind.

"No," he looked down at his hands, "but since our families are now related, I thought you and I might be more related. I mean, I am asking you to be my wife. I know we haven't known one another very long, but," he drew a deep breath, "we are leaving tomorrow, and I think we might do very well together."

Very well together, when just a day ago she had been dreaming of being passionately united with the only man she'd ever loved or desired. Desired! The thought of anyone else's hands besides Justin's, touching her made Georgie physically ill, but she smiled gently at Henry. After all, he was doing his best to be kind, to be a good son, a good brother, a good man. It wasn't his fault he wasn't Justin Appleton. "That is indeed most kind of you, and I am truly honored, but . . . well . . . I never thought to be married." It was not a complete lie; until Justin Appleton had appeared in her life, Georgie had been determined never to be married.

"Oh . . . I see. Verena said . . . well I had hoped, but if your mind is quite made up, I can understand." He paused, looking down at his feet for a moment, then glanced back up with the same self-deprecating expression that reminded Georgie so strongly of Verena, the Verena before she became Freddy's wife. "But we can still be friends then can we not? I would still like you to help me figure out what it is that is holding Pegasus back."

Was she hallucinating or did she detect just the slightest touch of relief in his tone? Yes. Georgie watched as he straightened and gestured towards the stables, he was relieved, and she was too, because no matter how upsetting the thought of anyone but Justin touching her, she didn't want to hurt this nice young man . . . and he was a nice young man. What other man would respect her wish to remain single? (Even though she could remember another man who had done just that). What other man would be so free of self-importance that he could accept rejection this gracefully?

"Of course, we can be friends, and I would be delighted to help Pegasus become all the horse he can be. Shall we go see him now? I believe we have just enough time to do so before we dress for dinner." They both headed back towards the stables with lighter steps, cheered by the prospect of helping Pegasus, and the next day, Georgie was able to say, with absolute honesty, that she looked forward to seeing Sanford again and hearing how the few suggestions she had made regarding Pegasus were working out.

Ashbourne settled back into its routine after the guests had left, a routine that included John, who had elected to stay on a few days before returning to London. After the bustle of the previous days, they were all looking forward to a little peace and quiet. Adrian went off to his horses, Juliette settled in the library with her sketchbook joined by John who soon buried himself in a book and Georgie who pored over *The Anatomy of the Horse*.

Serenity reigned as they sat in companionable silence until Juliette looked at the clock. "Gracious look at the time. No wonder I am longing for some tea. John? Georgie? I assume you could use some refreshment as well." They both nodded, and her hand was paused to ring the bell when Robert appeared.

"A letter has just come for Lady Georgiana," the footman responded to their inquiring looks.

"For me?" Georgie was mystified. She had just bid farewell to Verena. Who else would send her a letter, and an official-looking one at that? Surely something so official could not be bringing good news, especially when, as she could now see, it came from Mr. Prescott, a solicitor in Newmarket. She read quickly down the page, gasped, and then, as John and Juliette glanced up in surprise, she hurried out of the room.

Juliette looked over at John. "From her reaction, I gather it is a rather upsetting communication; I have never seen Georgie so white. Do you think one of us should go after her?"

"Ordinarily, I would say no. My sister, as you are so well aware, likes to take care of things on her own, but, in this case . . ." John paused as he recalled the tortured twist of her lips, "In this case, I . . ."

"Would you go? You are the one she would be most likely to turn to in distress, and you, well, you know how to offer comfort and solace."

John appreciated her confidence in him, but he was not sure there was much comfort and solace he could offer, not to someone as strong-minded as his sister. It would take a catastrophic revelation to upset her so much that she ran off in confusion. What he could do, however, was listen.

After some searching, he found Georgie seated in a secluded corner of the terrace, staring off over the fields, uncharacteristic tears streaming down her face. "He has given me Clinton House," she gasped as he sat down beside her.

John said nothing, taking her shaking hands in his as she fought for breath and control.

"I . . . I cannot believe he would do such a thing. So generous . . . so . . . when I was so very furious—am so very furious—with him." She paused as a myriad of expressions flitted across her face, from clench-jawed anger to frowning doubt, to quivering-lipped despair, at last bursting out, "Oh why, oh why did he do it? All of it?"

Still John sat quiet, his eyes fixed on her.

'He told me I should marry Sanford. Can you imagine? An American wanting me to *marry well*? For my sake, of course!" Georgie snorted. "I was furious with him. What right did he have to give me advice on my life, my happiness?" She pulled her hands away, twisting them in her lap as she tried to steady her breathing. "How could he, of all people?"

Now John heard the hurt and betrayal in her voice, but he sensed, knowing Justin, that it was not because he did not love Georgie enough as much as it was because he loved Georgie so much that he had urged her to marry Verena's brother. In fact, John had seen Verena and Justin speaking together on the terrace during the Venetian breakfast and, now as he reflected on it, the American had faded into the background immediately following that conversation and had left rather early. John had put it down to his feeling a little *de trop* as the only outsider in a family gathering, but now he wondered if Verena had hinted at something that had made Justin Appleton, American, democratic that he was, promote a similar aristocratic connection and family closeness by suggesting to Georgie what he thought would be a happy match.

"Georgie," he took her hands again, "I am sure he did it out of love for you. Whether or not he thought it was important for you to marry into a family of equal rank, I am *sure* he wanted you to marry into a family that was already happily married into yours, all, I might remind you, thanks to the benevolent manipulation on your part, of other people's lives."

"Perhaps," she did have the grace to look conscious as she accepted that. Then she raised that defiant Georgie Claverton chin, "but I still cannot tolerate a man who thinks he knows better than I do what is good for me."

She collapsed on his shoulder into sobs. "But he knows that I love Clinton House and he gave it to me, just for me, and he is gone back to America forever."

John held her in his arms until the sobbing had subsided. He sat her up straight and said, "Then, the best thing to do is to cherish that love he knows you feel for it, accept his gift, and honor his suggestion that you study with Mr. Tripp, and make Mr. Justin Appleton proud of all he has done for you."

Georgie gulped, wiped her eyes, gave a final sniff and favored her brother with a watery smile. "I will . . . and thank you, John."

CHAPTER 27

JUSTIN STARED AT THE LETTER IN HIS HANDS. Not only had his mother's parents disapproved of his father, as she'd always maintained, they hadn't known his father at all. His mother hadn't even been married! So now he was not just the son of someone unacceptable, he was a bastard! *But you are the true son of your stepfather, the son he never had,* she had written, *and that is all that matters, that and my reassurance that you were born out of love with the only man I ever truly loved. I kept your existence from him because I loved him so much. I know he would have done the honorable thing and married me, I know he would, but he needed to make a brilliant match to someone of his own exalted station so he could pursue the political career he planned, so he could make a difference in the world. By now I have been gone long enough that your heart will be softened and you can forgive me—I hope—but I also wanted you to know the truth and to know that your stepfather, who also knew the truth, is an extraordinary man worthy of all your love and respect because he truly loves and respects you, regardless of your birth.*

And then, there was the ring that had fallen out of the envelope—a gold signet ring with a small roll of paper in it which read, *This is the only thing of your father's that I possess. He gave it to me. I could not bear to give it back and lose everything of him that I had so now I pass it along to you, wear it and remember that you are born of love to a wonderful man.*

Justin slipped the ring on his finger, in memory of his mother and her love. She had always been a devoted mother and wife, but now, having experienced love himself, Justin realized that it was devotion he had witnessed, not love.

He flung open the library window, desperate for air to ease the ache in his chest and quell the feelings tearing him apart: shame for an existence that had ruined his mother's life and robbed him of a chance to know any true family, anger at his mother for having kept it from him, pity for what she had suffered, rejected by her family and alone until she had met his stepfather, and gratitude and admiration for that man's kindness and steadfastness in making them his family. What a truly amazing and generous man his stepfather had been. He had made Justin feel like a true son, giving him his care, affection, advice, education, and all the advantages a young man could ask, not to mention making him heir to the business he had founded and fostered. What man, natural father or not, could have done more?

He drank in the breeze pouring through the window, loosening the tightness in his chest and clearing his head. Even this, this manor house, this time in England, this chance to meet his true love, was a gift from his stepfather, and he owed it to him to honor him with his life, which meant returning to America and fulfilling his stepfather's dreams.

Just as Justin's throat tightened painfully at the thought of leaving, he was struck by a thought. Just as he was going to fulfill his stepfather's dreams, he would fulfill his own by making the dreams of the woman he cherished come true. He would give Clinton House to Georgie so she could live in a place she had always loved, being the equine caretaker and savior, she was meant to be—and he, Justin would find his own happiness in picturing her here, in her favorite room in her favorite house, poring over equine anatomy books and scholarly veterinary treatises.

There was no time like the present to make those dreams come true. Disregarding the lateness of the hour, Justin grabbed his hat, strode to the stables, saddled up Brutus and headed toward his solicitor in Newmarket, pausing just long enough to shout to Tim, who had raced to assist him, to ask Mr. Harrington to make all the necessary arrangements for Justin's immediate departure for London and then New York.

Thus, it was when John, determined to do what he could to ease the misery of his sister, rode over to Clinton House the next afternoon, he found the owner, well, its former owner, already gone to London.

"I am sorry you missed him, my lord." Jim Harrington led him into the library and offered him a seat while he sent for something to drink. "Is there some message you would like me to take to him? I shall be joining him for the voyage home after I have settled things here."

"No thank you. I had not realized he was leaving so soon. I had hoped for a few more chess games as I was under the impression, he was not leaving for America for another month at least. It was not an emergency, I trust," he probed gently, his eyes fixed on Justin's henchman's face.

"Well, yes, he did amend his plans somewhat after the letter he received the other day," the American admitted, weighing his words with care. "He had already received an invitation from Mr. Telford to attend the meeting of the Institution of Civil Engineers in London next week, which he planned to do, and then return here to settle things, but I told him I could take care of all that while he was in London, so there was no need for him to journey back here before we sailed."

John heard the hesitancy in the man's voice and saw the concern in his eyes. Something untoward had caused the change in plans, and Mr. Harrington was doing his level best to help and protect his friend. "Ah, then, that does make sense. No need for you to take a message; I shall catch up with him in London, as I am returning there myself in a day or so. What is his direction in London?"

"He is staying at Fladong's Hotel in Oxford Street. Him being in shipping and all, he finds the naval crowd there most congenial."

John rose and held out his hand. "Then I shall be going, but I wish you both a good journey home, and the best of luck in your canal-building endeavors."

"Thank you, my lord." Even Jim Harrington, American egalitarian that he was, knew that it was most unusual for a lord to offer his hand to someone that, even in America, would have been considered a servant by most people. But this man was something quite out of the common way. He saw things. Jim had felt his sympathetic, assessing gaze and knew that Lord John Claverton knew there was much more to the story than Jim had told him, and that Jim's oldest and closest friend was more troubled than Jim had seen him in his entire life.

It was that letter, that and the air of grim decision that had hung over Justin since he'd gone off to that party at Ashbourne, but the seriousness after the party had hinted at purpose, even if not happy purpose. The letter had brought what to Jim felt like unhappy confusion or loss, as though a boat had slipped its moorings and was drifting unpiloted away into the distance. The trip to London seemed more of an escape than a journey to attend a meeting, and there was nothing Jim could do about it except wait for the opportunity to help his friend wipe away the empty look in his eyes that was so unlike the tirelessly energetic, always focused on a goal, Justin Appleston he had known since boyhood.

All Jim could do was pack up their things at Clinton House and make sure it was set to welcome the new owner Justin had spoken of. Jim was not so surprised at that; Justin had always planned to sell Clinton House once he had visited it and seen the country where his mother had grown up. Still, it was a bit unexpected as Justin had seemed to be developing a fondness for the old place, not to mention his neighbors at Ashbourne, and to be very fond indeed of one of those neighbors. Jim had even begun to hope that Justin and Lord John's sister were on their way to reaching some sort of understanding, despite her being English and a lady and all, but after the party, all mention of Ashbourne and the Clavertons had ceased, much to Jim's sorrow, for he couldn't ever remember seeing Justin as relaxed and happy as he was after visiting the Clavertons at Ashbourne or having them at Clinton House. Now that happy, relaxed Justin was gone, replaced by a tense, lost stranger. Jim supposed it was all for the best, what with the vast difference in their lives and their countries, not to mention the separate endeavors to which Lady Georgiana and Justin were devoted, but it still was a sad thing to think of that friendship which seemed, from the little Jim had been able to observe, to have brought just as much happiness to Lady Georgiana Claverton as it had to Mr. Justin Appleton.

Jim returned to the arrangements he had been making before Lord John's appearance. He rather hoped that Lord John would call on Justin in London. The man seemed to have extraordinary powers of perception. You could just feel it when you talked to him, even if it were just a brief conversation. Perhaps he could somehow help his dear friend sort things out. Jim certainly hoped so.

John was hoping that too, so, cutting short his visit to Ashbourne, he headed back to London the next day. Juliette had been the only one to remark on his departure, Adrian being too involved with some issues with a new stud, and Georgie too busy with her own unhappy thoughts to notice. "We are sorry to see you leave so soon. You have something to attend to in London, I assume." She cast a knowing look in the direction of Clinton House whose owner had departed so precipitately. "I wish you Godspeed, and success in your endeavors." Her brow wrinkled in a frown that spoke volumes of her concern for Georgie's unhappiness.

CHAPTER 28

THUS, IT WAS THAT A FEW DAYS LATER, John strolled over to Fladong's from the rectory, inquired after Justin Appleton and sent up his card.

"Claverton," Justin greeted him with a firm handshake, but there was a question in those eyes which were unusually somber in a face, once full of vigor and energy, that was now gaunt, drained of all expression.

"I beg your pardon for intruding, but I had not expected you to be gone so soon after my arrival and hoped for at least another game of chess or two." John cocked his head, fixing Justin with that all-seeing, all-knowing look of his.

"Well, I had thought to stay a little longer, and I apologize to you and your family for not taking proper leave of you after your many kindnesses to me, but" he ran a hand through his hair, "but there were pressing things I realized I needed to attend to before departing for America."

The uncharacteristically nervous gesture caught John's eye, as did the signet ring on Justin's finger. He sat up straight. "I beg your pardon for my rather intrusive curiosity, but I do not remember your wearing that ring before." Then, seeing the faintest touch of red creeping into the pale cheeks, he strove for a lighter tone. "I thought you Americans rather frowned on such things as crests and all."

"Oh, er I have just received this . . . a letter from my mother, which only now found its way into my hands."

"The letter," John broke off gazing at him sympathetically. "Your friend, Mr. Harrington mentioned it. He is most concerned about you . . . as am I." He paused, looked down at the floor for a few moments, then glanced up with a self-deprecating smile. "I am a frightful busybody, you know. I expect it comes from ministering, or trying to minister, to my flock, and where the happiness of my family is concerned, I have no shame."

Justin sighed but offered no reply. On the other hand, he was not ordering John out of his room.

"You mean the world to my sister, and leaving her Clinton House was so kind, so generous, so thoughtful, as is everything you have done for her. She was in tears. I have never seen her cry before."

"I did not mean to hurt her. I would never hurt her for the world." Justin's voice was raw with agony. "Her happiness means everything to me, but . . . well . . . I am no good for her."

"I thought my sister-in-law had explained to you that while values mean a great deal in our family, rank does not necessarily." A ghost of a smile tugged at John's mouth. "My sister did not take kindly to having you, of all people, choose a husband for her."

"I know, I know," again Justin ran a hand through his hair, "And I was going to apologize for being so . . . so managing, even though Sanford would be an excellent match, but then . . ."

"But then, the letter," John prompted gently.

"The letter . . . I could not . . . not after that." Justin rose to begin pacing the room. "Not after I learned that not only that I was the son of someone my mother's family objected to, but that the person they objected to did not actually exist, that I am a bastard, the son of someone she could not marry, someone she wanted to protect so much she would not even tell *me* his name not even now a year after her death when she directed the letter be given to me. So, you see, I could not stay. I had to leave."

"Aaah." John rose to lay a hand on his shoulder. "I begin to understand. Now, if you do not mind, may I see that ring?"

Justin looked at him in astonishment. "What? Oh, very well." He pulled it off and handed it to John who glanced briefly at the seal and then back at Justin's face.

"Yes, I thought so. *Now* I see it all. If you will but remain here this evening, there is someone I want you to meet. Trust me," he squeezed Justin's shoulder reassuringly, "all will be well. I stake my reputation on it."

That evening when the hotel servant announced, "Two gentlemen to see you sir," Justin rose to find himself staring . . . into his very own eyes!

John edged around the visitor with a cautious smile. "Alfred Justin, Lord Wolverton, may I present to you Mr. Justin Appleton of America."

The amber eyes, so like Justin's filled with unshed tears as the man in front of him, a slightly grizzled version of himself, clasped Justin by the shoulders with shaking hands. "My son!" He choked.

"If I *am* your son, I am a bastard son," Justin blurted, too overwhelmed to think clearly.

"Balderdash! You're my son and that's all there is to it, and a fine fellow at that, according to Claverton here."

"Please be seated, my lord." Remembering his manners at last, Justin gestured toward a chair by the fire and brought out a decanter and glasses. "Brandy? Or I do have some excellent port."

"It's a brandy sort of meeting I would say." Lord Wolverton accepted a glass, took a deep swig, set it on the table next to him, and leaned forward, gesturing to the chair opposite. "Now tell me about yourself. Claverton here says you have the signet ring I gave Elizabeth . . . your mother."

With a speaking glance at John, who had the grace to look sheepish, Justin held out his hand to be examined.

It was several minutes before Lord Wolverton could speak. "She never told me. I never guessed. Believe me, son, I would have married her, but she would not have me speak of that sort of thing. She was determined for me to have a brilliant career in politics, even suggested the families I should marry into to advance that career." A tender smile lit his face. "A very clever woman, Elizabeth, but what would one expect from a young woman haunting Parkers bookshop in Oxford."

"Haunting a bookshop?"

"Yes, when I was a student there I too haunted that bookshop. I could not help noticing the rigorous tone of the books she kept leafing through. She told me she was there to pick up books for her father, a cleric of some sort, in a nearby parish, but the proprietor told me that her father's books tended toward religious tracts, not Locke and Hume and Adam Smith. I gather her father was rather hidebound and overbearing, and the proprietor had a soft spot for someone possessed of such a lively intelligence, so he let her linger as much as she wished, even suggesting other authors who might interest her."

A reminiscent smile softened the leonine features. "I had never met a woman who conversed like a human being instead of flirting, and who cared what I thought, not who I was. She encouraged my interest in politics and my desire to make the world a better place," he sighed, "something my father thought was naïve and self-indulgent. She and I would wander along the Cherwell, arguing and discussing, stopping now and again to revel in the beauty of the place, and . . . er . . . *other things*. I told her I loved her, and I know she loved me, but she was set on my marrying well to someone who could advance my career."

"Then, one day, she told me that we must stop seeing one another, that we were living in a fool's paradise, and that she was going to visit a relative so that she did not fall into the temptation of seeing me again. I could see her mind was made up, so I begged her not to forget me and I gave her the ring you now wear. I made her promise to send me that ring if she ever needed me, and told her I would come to her aid, no matter where she was or what had befallen her."

Lord Wolverton paused to catch his breath before giving his new-found son a searching look. "And now I am here, and it is not she who needs me, but her son who does. Don't poker up at me lad, I have heard the entire story from Claverton here, and I know my goddaughter, a fine girl, but strong-minded and stubborn. I gather you have fallen afoul of that strong-mindedness—through the best of intentions, of course. I think I can help with that."

"It is very kind of you, my lord, but she is better off without me. Begging your pardon, but not only is she from an important family, while I am an American commoner and a bastard. But a bastard with distinguished heritage," he amended with a self-deprecatory grin. "Still, we are from two different nations, two different worlds, and have two compelling, but different goals in life."

Lord Wolverton nodded slowly. "A perfectly sensible argument, but consider for a moment, an old man's perspective. Your *father's* perspective. He returned Justin's grin before growing serious. "If your mother had not tried to do *the right thing, the noble thing* I would have been a happy man. As it was, I married one of the women she suggested and had two daughters. My marriage was a respectful one, but lonely. My wife was an excellent mother and hostess, but I meant nothing to her except her duty, and when she died in childbirth many years ago, I was left with nothing but two well brought-up, dutiful daughters, and little else."

"Yes, I achieved my political dreams, but they were the dreams your mother and I, and" he glanced over at John, "his father shared them too. If it had not been for Roxburgh and his family," he smiled fondly at John, "I would be alone in this world. But now I have you!" Again, the amber eyes, so like Justin's, filled with tears. "I won't be as managing as Georgie was with her brother, or as you are trying to be with her, so I only offer my humble advice, which is that sometimes love and passion, though possibly reckless and unrealistic, are exactly what we need most. If your mother had allowed me to follow my love and passion, you would be the next Lord Wolverton—a much less interesting and useful life than you have now," he chuckled. "Please say you will think on it—not that Claverton and I haven't given you more than enough to think on—and now we shall leave you in peace."

Lord Wolverton rose, as did Justin, who trailed his guests to the door, where his father—how strange and magical to think of him as that— turned to him, his expression grave, "Please do one thing for me, allow me to introduce you to Roxburgh. Yes, yes," he waved a dismissive hand, "I know you have already met him, but I want to introduce you to him as my son and his daughter's suitor." With a provocative smile, he ducked out through the door before Justin could respond, John at his heels, closing the door behind him with an apologetic shrug.

Justin collapsed into his chair and gazed into the fire, his glass of brandy remaining untouched, his thoughts and feelings too jumbled to try to make sense of them. But as he sat there, they began to crystallize, not into coherent thought, but into a feeling, a feeling of joy. He was loved! He was wanted! He had been born out of love, and, unhappy as the results had been, it had all been inspired by love, his parents' love for one another, his mother's loving deception to protect his father, and, later on, her son's good name. He had thought her a distant and restrained woman, but now he realized that it was not so much distant as determined, determined to survive and make a way for both of them in the New World. And she had, and prospered, thanks to the unmitigated support and generosity of the man who had raised him and made him his heir.

Now he had two fathers! The more he thought about his mother and all that she must have suffered before going to work for his stepfather, the more his heart ached for her. As he sat there recalling those early days, he remembered the way he would sometimes catch her looking at him as though she were searching for something. Now he knew what that something was. She was searching for the image of her lost love, which she must have seen every time she looked into his eyes. Did it make her happy or sad? Even now, after all he had learned, he couldn't say for sure.

CHAPTER 29

Lord Wolverton was as good as his word, and the next morning a note was brought to Justin with his usual coffee, requesting him to visit his father at his residence in Berkeley Square at three in the afternoon, if that were not inconvenient for him.

It was not inconvenient. Aside from attending Telford's meeting, chatting with the seafaring men at Fladong's, and familiarizing himself with London so he could describe it to acquaintances back home, Justin had no pressing business—his most pressing business having been to leave Cambridgeshire behind him as quickly and completely as possible. But Cambridgeshire had followed him to London, and he was still trying to figure out what to make of it.

Once he had recovered from the shock of learning the identity of his true father, he had had time to reflect on what the man had said, and what the man had learned from bitter experience. If he thought Justin should toss aside his noble plans of sacrifice and pursue the course of true love, perhaps Justin should consider it. After all, if his real father saw Justin as Georgie's (his goddaughter, no less) suitor, then perhaps Justin should indeed reconsider. But would Georgie? He knew her pride and determination. He knew how much he had not only insulted her intelligence and independence, but perhaps he had hurt her badly as well. It was a lot to account for. Still, the prospect of seeing Georgie again, of talking with her, begging her to take him back, filled his heart with hope. Now all he needed was a bit of encouragement.

When Justin was ushered into the library of Lord Wolverton's imposing Berkeley Square residence, it was to discover the Duke of Roxburgh chatting companionably with his old school chum. Roxburgh glanced from Justin to Wolverton and back again, recognition dawning. Lord Wolverton laughed. "Now you see why I invited you here, Roxburgh. I wanted to introduce you to my son, Mr. Justin Appleton of New York." The man was bursting with such pride that it took a moment for Justin to swallow the lump in his throat. He turned to Roxburgh, "Your Grace."

"I think you had better call me Roxburgh if you are thinking of asking for my daughter's hand."

"Whaaaat?" Justin looked at his father who chuckled, rubbing his hands together.

"Sorry, lad. I have already been making a case for you as a serious suitor for my god-daughter's hand. I simply neglected to mention to Roxburgh, here, that I was not an entirely disinterested party."

"Wolverton has always played his cards close to his chest, but this is the closest I have ever experienced," the duke chuckled in return. "But come, sit down. Make your case to me. I already know from various other family members that you and my Georgie have formed a rare friendship indeed, and that you were the inspiration and the impetus behind her apprenticeship to Mr. Tripp." He paused a moment, lost in thought. "I only wish someone had done the same for my wife. They are very like, you know, Georgie and her mother—clever, hard-working, and passionate about the things they care about, though Amelia's passion is dogs rather than horses. At any rate, you have sized up Georgie to perfection and treated her as an equal—a rare quality in any man, and one I consider necessary in anyone asking for my daughter's hand in marriage."

The duke fixed Justin with a sharp-eyed look. "Well? You *are* asking for her hand, are you not? Do not tell me that two of my sons, my daughter-in-law, and my oldest friend are mistaken."

"Ah . . . no . . . er, sir, er, your Grace. It is just that I have made such a mull of it by suggesting to her a more eligible suitor that I fear she will no longer have anything to do with me."

"Oh, Sanford," the duke dismissed Verena's brother with a wave of his hand, "nice enough, but dull, very dull, and no spine at all. She would be bored within a fortnight and have done him in within a year."

"Besides, welcome as I have been made to feel here, I am an American."

"And have substantial business interests there, I hear. Shipping interests, I gather." He shot Justin another penetrating look and Justin's hopes rose.

"Yes, I do," he replied firmly. "And I have been investigating the use of steam engines in powering ships across the Atlantic, as my father's friend, Robert Fulton, has done in America."

"There, you, see?" The duke smiled broadly at Wolverton, "I *knew* John had mentioned something about steam-powered ships. Clever fellow, John . . . for a man of the cloth. I expect that if you work on it, that soon it will not take a great deal longer to get from New York to London than it would from London to some godforsaken holding in Scotland."

Indeed, Justin thought, the future was looking brighter and brighter, and his potential father-in-law increasingly intelligent.

"You are in the right of it your Grace, and with the right weather it could only be a matter of a few weeks' voyage from New York to London, but favorable as your argument is about the distance not being a hindrance, there is a more important issue, which is your daughter's justifiable resentment of my interference."

The duke nodded. "You are right to consider it. Georgie has her standards, and she is a force to be reckoned with—not to mention stubborn—and the quickest way to ruin her favorable impression of you is to interfere in her life to suggest she do something for her own good, especially if it is something you, rather than she, conceived of. I quite understand her irritation with your pushing Sanford on her. On the other hand, you not only encouraged her to follow her passion in caring for horses, you bought her equine anatomy books and arranged for her to study with Mr. Tripp—which is, in truth, a great deal more managing than recommending the son of her best friend as a prospective suitor—and she not only didn't get angry with you for your suggestions, but she was grateful for your encouragement." The duke rubbed his hands together. 'I think I see the beginning of a convincing argument. Wolverton, you and I will have to talk to her . . . delicately, of course."

Lord Wolverton turned to his son. "You see why he is such a force in Parliament?"

Justin nodded, thinking, *and extremely well informed.* "I shall be most grateful for any advice and assistance. I am in debt to both of you for your generous support."

The duke waved this aside. "Think nothing of it. Wolverton and I haven't had such a challenge in years. Politics has been rather dull lately and this makes us feel young again, eh, Augie?"

Justin's father laughed. "Yes, it does. Now the real work begins. Convincing your daughter to change her mind is trickier than taking on all of Parliament. I think Justin and I can handle this now he has your permission to address your daughter but do stand by as we may have to call you in should we need reinforcements."

"I await your instructions, should you need me." The duke rose and held out his hand to Justin, who had also risen. "Good luck, lad."

"Thank you, your Grace," Justin smiled ruefully, "I shall need it."

CHAPTER 30

THE RETURN JOURNEY TO CAMBRIDGESHIRE was a pleasant one, Justin and his father swapping stories of their lives the entire way.

Lord Wolverton nodded approvingly as they rumbled over the bridge, across the moat, and into the courtyard of Clinton House. "A venerable property, my boy. I can see why my goddaughter is so taken with it."

Jim Harrington came hurrying out at the sound of a vehicle arriving in the courtyard, his jaw dropping as the carriage door opened, steps were let down and the occupants emerged. "Justin, I didn't expect you . . . you and . . . your?"

"Father. You are quite correct." Lord Wolverton stepped forward. "You must be Harrington. Justin told me you were a clever fellow." The grin accompanying these words told anyone who happened to see it, how much he was enjoying his dramatic entrance.

"May I present you to Lord Wolverton, Jim." Justin moved over to stand next to his father. "And yes, he *is* my father, my natural father."

"*Father* is the only word you need, lad," Lord Wolverton growled.

Recovering from his astonishment as he looked from one ruddy-headed, amber-eyed gentleman to the other, Jim reveled in the unmistakable affection between the two of them. "Then I gather there has been a change in plans."

"Yes, I told Kincade Webb to sail without us."

"Justin has returned to take up his courtship of my goddaughter."

"Goddaughter?"

"Yes, Lady Georgiana Claverton. Roxburgh and I are old school chums, you see."

As if that explained everything, Jim thought, his mind awhirl. "But . . ." his brow wrinkled.

"But my boy insulted her by suggesting a more suitable claimant to her hand, and now there is the devil to pay, which is why I have come to help him reclaim his place in her affections. You are in the right of it, there is some cause for unease, but we shall work it out. Now," Lord Wolverton nodded in towards Justin, "please show me your place, lad."

They proceeded into the Great Hall while Jim, still shaking his head in wonder at the turn of events, along with Sam Crimmins and another lad from the stables took care of the horses and the luggage.

"And tomorrow," Justin's father set down his glass of after-dinner brandy sometime later as they sat before the fire in the library, "we shall beard them all in their den, or at least we shall pay a visit to Ashbourne, and you will lay your case before my god-daughter while I stand by should you need assistance."

"Lord Wolverton to see you, my lady," Wilson announced the next afternoon as Juliette and Georgie sat in the library studying a sketchbook in one case and equine anatomy texts in the other.

"Wolverton? Strange he didn't let us know he was coming," Juliette mused.

Georgie, who had glanced out the window overlooking the drive, and caught sight of the familiar carriage, gasped and hurried out of the room.

Before Juliette could even wonder at her sister-in-law's hasty exit, the butler ushered not one, but two gentlemen into the room.

"Lord Wolverton." Juliette rose. She looked from one man to the other. "And Mr. Justin Appleton. Or, I should say, Alfred *Justin*, Lord Wolverton," she amended, smiling.

"You never miss a trick, do you Lady Adrian." Lord Wolverton chuckled. "May I present to you my *son*, Mr. Justin Appleton of New York."

The pride in his voice and the glow of happiness about him brought tears to Juliette's eyes. "John," she whispered, "I should have known! I don't know how my brother-in-law does it, but he sees things the rest of us do not."

"That he does," Lord Wolverton agreed.

"Goodness, how rag-mannered of me," Juliette waved a hand toward two chairs, "please do sit down and tell me everything . . . though," she glanced at Justin, "I expect you might like to go find Georgie. I believe she is in the stables, which is where she usually goes when she is faced with a situation she cannot handle."

"You *are* as deep a one as John, I would say," Lord Wolverton sat down in the offered chair as Justin headed off to find Georgie. "Now, ordinarily I would make polite inquiries about the health and happiness of you, your husband, and your son, but I am too full of my own news. May I tell you all about it?"

"Please do!" Juliette leaned forward, her face alight with curiosity.

As expected, Justin found Georgie in Nero's stall, vigorously brushing out his mane and muttering furiously in his ear.

The words were completely muffled, but Justin could just imagine them, *Pompous, interfering American! Who does he think he is, telling me what to do?* "Geo . . . er, Lady Georgiana . . ."

The vigorous brushing ceased. "I have nothing to say to you."

"I know you don't beyond, *Get out of my sight, you filthy varlet.*" *Filthy varlet?* Where had that come from? They said desperation was the mother of invention, and it was proving to be true. "I know you don't have anything to say to me, and I don't deserve to have you speak to me, pompous interfering American that I am." He really was doing rather well with his choice of vocabulary today. "But I," Justin bit his lip, "have something to say to you."

Georgie turned around, blue eyes blazing with fury. It was the lip, awkwardly caught between his teeth that got to her, so, instead of planting him a facer, as she longed to do, she took a breath, and drew herself up proudly. "Out with it and be quick about it. Nero doesn't like his grooming interrupted."

"First, I am very, very sorry for upsetting you. I was so intent on trying to help that . . . that . . . I didn't realize how incredibly arrogant it was for me to suggest a thing to you when you are perfectly capable of—more than capable of—managing your own life."

Georgie's rigid stance relaxed just the tiniest bit. Most men never apologized, and as apologies went, it *was* rather a decent one.

"What I meant by doing it was that I love you, and I wanted what was best for you," he paused, swallowed hard, and whispered, "no matter what it cost me."

The blue blaze left her eyes, replaced by a questioning look—not a complete softening, but at least a willingness to hear more."

"What he meant was, he was trying to be a valiant fool, not counting the cost of losing the thing most precious in the world to him, a cost he would not be able to comprehend until twenty or so years hence." Lord Wolverton stepped around the stall to stand next to Justin. 'So, I told him what that cost would be."

Georgie took one look at the two of them and raised her hand to her lips as all the color drained from her face.

"Georgie!" Without thinking, Justin rushed to her side to offer a steadying arm as she sank onto a bale of hay.

"I think . . . I think you two have some explaining to do." She tried to summon a ferocious frown but failed entirely as she looked from one man to the other.

Justin fell to his knees at her feet. "The last I saw of you; I had no idea that Lord Wolverton existed. The day I sent you the deed to Claverton, I had just received a letter from my mother, to be delivered a year after her death, admitting that she never had been married to my father, but had gone to America to avoid the shame of being an unmarried woman with child. She said that marriage to the man who was my father, a man whose name she still refused to divulge, was out of the question because of his exalted rank and the damage that such a marriage would do to his political career. She did, however, leave me the signet ring he had given her as a pledge of his love. It was your brother, John, who figured it out."

"And gave me back my precious son."

Georgie glanced up at her godfather to see his leonine face softened by a tender smile, his eyes glistening with unshed tears, a man completely unlike her driven, ambitious godfather. "Oh my."

"And that is why I have interrupted the perfectly credible job my son was doing to beg you to reconsider his suit. You see," Lord Wolverton settled next to Georgie on the hay bale, "Elizabeth thought she was doing what was best for me by leaving and forcing me to marry one of the women she considered most likely to advance my career. Only she wasn't advancing my career. I would have done brilliantly, no matter what, "he smiled wryly, "but I was missing her and lonely for her my entire life.

Yes, I have two wonderful daughters and their children, but it is a family bound together by duty rather than the love that binds your family. That is why I urge you and my son to consider the passion and not the practicality, or, I should say, let love conquer all. I see the way he looks at you with his heart in his eyes. I know what that feels like, and I have been missing it every day of my life for the last thirty years."

"It was love at first sight," Justin declared.

Glancing at his goddaughter, Lord Wolverton laughed as an uncharacteristic blush flooded her face. "Oh my, you too?"

"Well," Justin grinned, "she and her groom came to deliver an invitation to call at Ashbourne. No one answered the door, so she sought me out . . . in my smithy which was the only place with any signs of life."

"Your smithy? That sounds interesting. You'll have to tell me more later. But go on, lad, you were saying."

"She found me hammering a piece I was working on, and . . ."

"And" his father continued triumphantly as his god-daughter's blush deepened, ". . . you were appropriately clad for the job you were doing, not a jacket . . . and, undoubtedly rather disheveled." Georgie's face was scarlet by now. He laughed. "You two best be wed quickly. No waiting for the banns to be read. Your brother John must help him procure a special license. And now I will leave you two to sort the rest out." Lord Wolverton rose, kissed his goddaughter on the cheek and headed out of the stall, pausing only to say, "And, by the way, my son has your father's permission. Take a look at the letter in his pocket."

"You have Papa's permission?"

"Even in America, a man feels it incumbent upon him to ask the parents of his beloved for their blessing."

"Oh . . . oh . . .," Georgie looked down at her hands, "I do not know what to say."

"For what must be the first time in your life." Justin looked deep into her eyes as he brushed aside a stray curl. "Don't say anything, just let me hold you."

She nodded slowly as he pulled her to him, cradling her against his chest and stroking her hair. At last she raised her head, her eyes full of tears. "I don't know what to think. I am so very angry at you, but I missed you desperately, and I will miss you even more if you leave me and go back to America, as you should, to take care of your business."

"And *now* who is the managing one," he teased. "We will sort it out, together, because that is where we belong, together." He pressed his lips to hers as her mouth opened beneath his, drinking in his strength and passion. His father was right, they could not be married soon enough, was her last conscious thought as one large hand drifted to her breast, and her whole body rose up to meet him.

Epilogue—Six Months Later

THEY STOOD, THE THREE OF THEM, Georgie, Justin, and his father, on the terrace of the Appleton family estate overlooking the Hudson River, drinking the magnificent view.

"Beautiful, simply beautiful." Encircled by Justin's arms, Georgie gazed in awe across the broad river to the hills beyond.

"A very fine establishment indeed," Wolverton agreed, "not to mention the fleet of ships and the docks. A most impressive enterprise you have here, my son. It makes me feel young again, what with the sea voyage and the trip up this mighty river. And to think you are planning to make that sea voyage a mere nothing with your steamship plans. And you, my dear," he turned to his goddaughter, now daughter-in-law, "have plans of your own. How fortunate that Mr. Tripp's fellow veterinarian from the army has come to try his fortunes in America where he can repay Justin, here, for setting him up in business by taking on his wife as an apprentice."

"But before he builds his steamships, Justin must finish the canal building that brought him to England in the first place, along with his inheritance of Clinton House, of course. The part he has played in the construction of the locks connecting Schenectady with the Hudson River, according to his designs for their improved mechanisms is just beginning." Georgie favored her new husband with a proud smile.

"Just beginning, perhaps, but I want you to take me for a trip on the finished part of the canal, all two hundred and twenty miles of it," Wolverton added. "I am longing to see some of this vast country you keep talking about."

"It will be such an adventure." Georgie agreed.

"You? You are coming with us. But . . . but . . .," her godfather looked at her in some concern.

He was brought up short by her fierce frown. "No child of mine," Georgie snorted, as she smoothed her hand over a belly that was only slightly beginning to increase, "is ever going to be denied the chance for adventure, and no child of mine is ever going to say no to that chance," she declared in no uncertain terms.

Justin smiled as he drew her closer into his arms. "A force to be reckoned with, and that's why I married her."

Georgie smiled up at him. "We both are."

Lord Wolverton guffawed. "I never thought the day would come when Georgie met with her match, and I am glad I lived to see it . . . and my beloved son." He laid a proud hand on Justin's shoulder. "Make those ships of yours eat up the miles, lad, because I plan to visit you often.

I STARTED WRITING TO KEEP MYSELF FROM GOING CRAZY hunting for a library job in the awful job market 40 years ago, and I discovered I loved it. A few months later, I got a job as a young adult librarian in what is now my local public library and finished a book over the year, setting it aside for five years while I concentrated on work (by then, Head of Reference and later Assistant Director) when I started contacting a few publishers who quickly responded with standard rejection letters until Penguin misplaced the manuscript and felt so apologetic they offered a two book contract. I published a book a year, and one reissue, for 16 years until they closed the line. Those books are still selling steadily as e-books for Belgrave House. In 2021 Camel Press brought out, *Mistress of Fashion*, the first book in my Ladies of Independent Means trilogy. *Mistress of Herself* is the first book in a duology sequel to Ladies of Independent Means. Retired from full-time library work, I continue part-time in the best job of all, reference librarian in a very busy library.

www.ingramcontent.com/pod-product-compliance
Lightning Source LLC
Chambersburg PA
CBHW010544100726
47903CB00011B/3128